ALL ABOUT MAX,

and something about Moose, a girl named Mitzi, a couple of mongrels called Moxie and Mojo, a bunch of old people, and the mysterious map of Measley Manor.

By
Barbara Brooks Wallace

Pangea Press

All About Max

and something about Moose, a girl named Mitzi, a couple of mongrels called Moxie and Mojo, a bunch of old people, and the mysterious map of Measley Manor.

First Pangea Press edition.
ISBN-13:978-0-9982542-6-5

An imprint of Pangea
Dana Point, California 92629

Dedication

For Jim, Boo, Bizzy, Big & Little John, Cheryl, & Blythe (my O.A.O.P.P.)

With love and a zillion thanks for all you do!

 Chapter I

In which we meet Max, known at the moment by his full name, Maximilian, his very rich parents, his despicable friend Pencival, his servants, pets and life in general.

O nce upon a time, (it's not necessary to this story to know exactly when), there was a boy named Maximilian Pettigrew Westmorington Bassford Thorndike Finstersill Smith the Fifth. His father, Maximilian P.W.B.T.F. Smith the Fourth, naturally, was enormously rich.

Therefore, it followed that young Maximilian Five was enormously rich as well. Or at least he would be some day when Maximilian Four was no longer around. As Five was an only boy, not to mention an only child, he would of course inherit it all. Every last penny, nickel, dime and dollar, not to mention every last euro, yen, yuan, peso, pound, rouble, rial, and loonie. Maximilian Four was indeed VERY rich!

Five wasn't *exactly* quite as rotten spoiled obnoxious as he might be from being the only child of such wealthy parents who gave him anything and everything he ever wanted, although he came perilously close to it. The *"exactly"* factored in because he did have two un-rotten-spoiled traits. The main one was that he was really and truly nice to animals and had never teased or tormented one even when he was very little and didn't know any better.

From a very early age, Five insisted that animals talked to him, including Sir Launcelot and Lady Guinevere, the very elegant (also snooty) Borzois (purebred, naturally!) that were the family dogs. Well, he talked to *them*, at any rate, and was quite certain he read their minds and knew *exactly* what they were saying to him.

Of course, nobody believed the thing about talking to animals. His parents, even though they thought this was cute, didn't really believe it either. Who would?

Maximilian was smart enough to figure out (actually, he was probably too smart and clever for his own good) that people were mostly nice to him because his father was so enormously rich, and some day he would be as well. Even when he was acting rotten spoiled obnoxious, and he was certain they wanted to take him over their knees and whale the daylights out of him, they would still be nice to him. People especially in this category were Mrs. Pinkerpon, the family cook, Binge, the family butler, and Gridlock, the family chauffeur who drove him to his posh private school every day, shop clerks in the posh stores where his family shopped, and even his teachers at Ballyhoo's, his posh private school. They were certainly all polite, at any rate.

But animals were another matter. They loved you and were nice to you no matter how rich your father was, or how rotten spoiled you behaved. They loved you just because you were you. He was certain that even Sir Launcelot and Lady Guinevere loved him. Of course, being elegant (purebred, of course, as mentioned), Borzois, they were rather snooty about showing affection. They never leaped on you and slobbered all over you like some general, all-round, non-snooty dogs are often likely to do. Still, Maximilian Five was certain they loved him.

After all, they were animals, weren't they? And hadn't he even asked them, each one separately?

"Do you love me, Sir?" asked Maximilian.

"*Yes!*" replied Sir Launcelot.

"Do you love me, Lady?" asked Maximilian.

"*Of course, silly boy!*" replied Lady Guinevere.

(Animals' replies and general conversations throughout this book are noted in italics to indicate that they are only understood by Maximilian. The author assumes that everyone reading this book knows what "italics" are, or can at least figure it out. Thank you.)

At any rate, it was funny how Maximilian had known about animal love from the time he was old enough to know anything.

Once, when he was still quite small, he snatched his hand away from his nanny to run out into a dangerously busy street to rescue a kitten. His nanny was fired for having let go of him, but his parents had a medallion of solid 18k gold made in his honor. It had his face and name on one side and on the other a kitten rampant. It was displayed in a glass case on their fireplace mantel.

Maximilian Five's second un-rotten-spoiled trait was...was...well, the truth was that he didn't really have a second one. Unless you could consider that way deep down inside him, he probably suspected that he was rotten spoiled obnoxious. He didn't know why that was, though, or what to do about even if he wanted to. Which he really didn't.

Actually, he was so used to being it that he couldn't imagine himself being anything else. Besides, he couldn't help remembering that his one great un-rotten-spoiled deed had certainly won him a gold medal, but it had also got his favorite nanny fired, and people who saw the medal snickered at it behind his parents' backs. So what was the use? Why even bother to try?

Maximilian had two whole rooms to himself in their six-bedroom penthouse apartment in the city. One room was the one which held his bed and his desk. The other was for all his toys. He had just about every expensive and even not-so toy ever manufactured. The room was bulging at the seams with them, and yet more and more kept being added. Most of his toys were because his parents traveled a lot. Both of them, and without *him.* That was the explanation behind so many of the toys.

Every time they left, especially when they both left at the same time, Maximilian Five managed to stage a crying fest, and giving him a toy made his parents feel less guilty. Maximilian played this game to the hilt. He knew that all these histrionics (which means a deliberate display of emotion for effect) didn't make them change their minds about leaving him, but he had figured, also at an early age, he might as well get something out of it. Although he had outgrown the tantrums he had when very small, his later crying scenes were worthy of a Hollywood Oscar award.

Maximilian P.W.B.T.F. Smith the Fourth had every penny, nickel, dime and dollar, not to mention euro, yen, yuan, peso, pound, rouble, rial, and loonie invested all over the world, and so had to go visit these investments, which meant leaving home frequently. Most recently, though, he had sold out all those many investments, every single last one, and plopped every euro, yen, yuan, peso, pound, rouble, rial and loonie into one huge, enormous project which actually had him leaving home even more frequently.

"My father has bought an island," Maximilian bragged to his erstwhile friend Pencival one Saturday morning. The word "erstwhile" (which means formerly) is used in referring to Pencival because he was more often erst than not. At that moment, it happened to be *not,* so Pencival and Maximilian were on speaking terms. Pencival was also a Ballyhoo boy, and about as rotten spoiled as Maximilian. Their family chauffeurs ferried the boys back and forth to each other's penthouses to play. This usually happened when one or the other had a new toy to show off. A lot of their conversations often consisted of bragging.

"What's he going to do with an island?" asked Pencival.

"Build a whole city on it," replied Maximilian. "There are even going to be a couple of skyscrapers. They're practically both built already."

"Skyscrapers on an island sounds pretty loony to me," said Pencival, who, Maximilian guessed, was probably eaten up with jealousy. Pencival's own father was terribly rich, but he got that way manufacturing and selling plumbing supplies and fixtures like bathtubs and toilets. Anybody dealing with bathtubs and such boring (even though highly necessary) things as toilets would never have had the imagination to do anything as daring as buying an island and building skyscrapers on it.

"Where is this crazy island?" asked Pencival.

"In the South Pacific," said Maximilian.

Pencival had to take a moment to come up with a zinger to shoot off about this. "So what's anyone supposed to do with themselves on an island in the South Pacific, just sit around watching the coconut trees grow? Ho hum!"

"Oh no! This is going to be a *resort* island called Rainbow's End. Only instead of a pot of gold, there'll be lots of entertainment by big bands and movie stars, and gambling. Well, that's for when you're not going swimming, or snorkeling, or deep sea fishing, or hanging around on the white sand beaches, or eating in five star restaurants," said Maximilian, who knew all about things like five-star restaurants. He knew Pencival did as well.

"Oh, and there's even going to be fireworks every night," he said. He knew Percival was crazy about fireworks.

Of course, Maximilian was making all of it up once he got past the word "resort", but why let Pencival know that? Besides, knowing his father, it was probably mostly, if not entirely true.

Anyway, all this was a lot for Pencival to chew on. It took him even longer to come up with another zinger of a reply. "So how is anyone expected to get there?" He snickered. "Swim? Ha! Ha!"

"Oh, they'll just get there in one of the two ocean liners my father is building, or fly in one of his fleet of airplanes," said Maximilian, who didn't have to make this up. It was exactly what he'd heard his father say, and it shut Pencival right up. The son of a man who sold plumbing fixtures, bathtubs and toilets was no match against two ocean liners and a fleet of airplanes.

"So when are we going to eat?" Pencival said, and actually managed to produce a fake yawn. He had clearly run out of zingers, so the next best thing was to pretend he wasn't interested in any old island. Maximilian wasn't fooled for a minute, but there was no use rubbing Pencival's nose in this island business any further.

"Aren't you interested in seeing the latest first?" asked Maximilian.

"Well, yeah, that's why I'm here, isn't it?" said Pencival. "Where'd it come from, China?"

"Actually Germany," said Maximilian. "And more like 'they'. That's where my mother was when she had them sent to me."

These latest gifts to Maximilian explain why Maximilian Fifth's mother was away from home so much traveling. She wasn't with Maximilian Fourth at all, but was traveling by herself as she always did.

The reason for all this traveling was that, not content with just having a busy social life going to teas and lunches, and being chairman or secretary of charities, and little theatres, and art societies, she also ran a business. This was a store called The Golden Truffle.

Maximilian never thought this name made much sense as everyone knows truffles are candy, but though the store did sell some VERY expensive *bona fide* (which is a dandy Latin expression meaning actually) truffles in assorted flavors, it mostly sold gifts and art objects and doodads imported from all over the world. It was a VERY posh store, and its pink gift boxes with the gold lettering, were so well known that anyone seeing one knew at once where what was packed inside came from. At any rate, while Maximilian Four was traveling around the world overseeing his many investments, Mrs. Maximilian Four traveled around the world buying things for The Golden Truffle.

Now Pencival's mother also had a busy social life going to teas and lunches, and being chairman or secretary of charities, and little theatres, and art societies, but still, she was the wife of someone who sold bathtubs and toilets. And most especially, she did *not* run a posh business whose pink boxes with the gold letters were becoming legendary, and even whose truffles Pencival adored. He had to use every power he possessed to pretend to Maximilian he though they were yucky. So Maximilian stopped offering them to him, and Pencival was sadly learning the meaning of "cutting off his nose to spite his face."

"So what is it you have to show me?" he asked Maximilian.

Maximilian lifted off a box from his overloaded shelf of boxes, and handed it to Pencival.

"This is just a bunch of building blocks!" said Pencival, managing to produce a very nice sneer.

"Not just any building blocks," said Maximilian. "They're skyscrapers. I can set up a city with them."

"So they're still just building blocks," said Pencival. "Is that all I came over to see?"

"No," said Maximilian, trying to sneer right back at Pencival. The word "trying" is because he was never able to out-sneer Pencival, no matter how hard he practiced sneering in front of his bathroom mirror. Sneering really is an art form, and they should give classes in it. "I suppose you didn't hear me say 'they' instead of 'it'. I've got something else."

Maximilian pulled another box from his shelf. "I suppose you've heard of Quadrilla?" He knew very well that Pencival hadn't.

"Oh, sure," said Pencival. "But it's been such a long time since I've played it. You'd better tell me."

Quadrilla was such a new kind of game that Pencival couldn't possibly have played it a long time ago. But Maximilian decided he wouldn't mention it. Pencival, such as he was, was his only friend. No point in ruining the relationship any further. So Maximilian explained all about it, and they ended up getting so engrossed in playing the game, that Maximilian rang the bell for Binge to bring lunch to his room.

"So what did you think of Quadrilla?" Maximilian asked Pencival when it was time for him to leave.

"Oh, it was okay," said Pencival, who wouldn't have admitted to liking it for his life. But then he tipped his hand by making the big mistake of asking, "Is your mother going to send you anything more from Germany?" He did produce a credible bored yawn, though.

"No," said Maximilian. "She already left Germany to go to Rainbow's End."

"I thought your parents never traveled together," said Pencival.

This was true. They didn't. That was because in case a plane went down, it would still leave one parent to look after Maximilian Five. That was no big secret.

"They're *not* going together," said Maximilian. "My father's already there, and she she's going to meet him. I'll get to see it when I go there to spend the summer."

"Well, I hope the island doesn't sink," said Pencival in a tone of voice that hoped just the opposite.

"Oh, no fear of that," said Maximilian. "My father had dozens of the smartest engineers and scientists, and even deep sea divers checking it out. It's the safest place in the world. You'll have to have to come visit me this summer."

"I might," said Pencival, trying to look bored. "And again I might not. Who knows?"

He didn't produce a sneer, however, as there wasn't anything really to sneer about. And though Pencival was a lot of unpleasant things, one thing he was not was stupid. There was no point in cutting off his nose to spite his face over a possible trip to this fantastic island where there would even be fireworks very night. Pencival had already ruined himself over the truffles.

As it turned up, something was actually happening right at that very moment that was to determine whether Pencival was ever to go by plane, or ship, or on the back of a whale, or any other way to Rainbow's End. And, as soon will be revealed, it had nothing to do with how many tubs or toilets his father sold, in case anyone was wondering if the cost of the trip might have anything to do with this.

No, it was something else entirely.

Chapter II

In which we learn why Pencival would no doubt never get
to visit Maximilian at rainbow's end, which has nothing
to do with his father not being able to sell enough tubs
and toilets to pay for him to get there but another reason
entirely.

Now there is a poem by a famous Scottish poet that says "The best laid schemes o' mice and men gang aft agley." What this means, of course, is that no matter how carefully you plan and plot, things often can get all fouled up. That's probably how he would have put it if the word "fouled" had been in popular use in those days.

Maximilian Pettigrew Westmorington Bassford Thorndike Finstersill Smith the Fourth knew all about the meaning of things ganging aft agley. Therefore, he had no intention of risking a single penny, nickel, dime, and dollar, not to mention one euro, yen, yuan, peso, pound, rouble, rial, or loonie on some harebrained scheme ganging anywhere that wouldn't safely guarantee the doubling, trebling, or even quadrupling every penny, nickel, dime, etc. etc. etc.

11

So Maximilian P.W.B.T.F. Smith the Fifth was absolutely right when he told Pencival that his father had hired dozens of the smartest engineers and scientists, and deep-sea divers to check out the island where he intended to build and run the most fantastic resort ever imagined by anyone in their wildest dreams. He had scoured every university and science laboratory and oceanographic institution to hire these people. They were the best in the world, and every last one had assured him that the island for Rainbow's End was one hundred per cent safe for this magnificent venture.

Alas, Maximilian P.W.B.T.F. should have paid more attention to that famous poem.

It turns up there was some teeny, tiny infinitesimally (meaning, of course, which could only be seen under a powerful microscope) small thing he hadn't considered. Well, who would? Who would have thought that a tiny sea creature crawling on the bottom of the ocean might have such astonishing power that it could be the cause of what subsequently happened. At least, that's what everyone *thought* must have been the cause, though, to be sure, they were only guessing.

But also, who would have thought that way, way, way, as far way as you could get at the very bottom of the ocean, where whales and sharks and tuna and swordfish, eels and jellyfish had been swimming and floating for centuries over quiet ripples of sand far from any stormy waves overhead, there was a tiny infinitesimally small crack. (Infinitesimally, of course, also meaning, it was so tiny that only a magician could have found it). Seriously, it was *that* tiny.

Sadly, among all the engineers and scientists and deep-sea divers there was not one single magician. This was the one thing Maximilian Four hadn't thought of in the matter of ganging agley. Well, once again, who would? How many magicians do universities, science laboratories, and oceanographic institutions employ?

And, after all, who would think that after all those centuries of just being a mere (*very* mere, indeed!) tiny crack in the ocean floor, some itty bitty, eency tweency creature would crawl over it, and unbelievably cause it to shift a little. Then the crack, quite on its own, having discovered (one can only suppose) it could do this, enjoyed doing it so much, it shifted some more.

The tiny sea creature (if that was indeed what did it) was probably long gone, but the crack it had crawled over grew and grew. It ended up being an enormous crack which, when it finally shifted one last fearful time, caused the island sitting peacefully on top of it to shudder and shake. Shuddering and shaking of the land, as everyone knows, is an earthquake.

So that's what happened to Rainbow's End, a stupendous, bone-cracking, dilly of an earthquake. Everything, but *EVERYTHING* came crashing down, and all the hotels and casinos and restaurants, and what was left of them sank into the ocean along with most of the island. The island did have some small hilly spots, which was really fortunate, as we shall see.

What was also fortunate, was that Maximilian Four had had just about all the workers on the island airlifted back to the mainland for that weekend. There were only enough people left to prepare some five-star gourmet meals and change the bed sheets in the fancy tent set up as a hotel room. Maximilian Four wanted the island practically to himself and Mrs. Four. This was the first time she had allowed herself a vacation from The Golden Truffle, her travels, and Maximilian Five, and they were going to enjoy a second honeymoon with a whole island almost all to themselves. It was really a very romantic idea.

And then the earthquake happened. Fortunately, the few people left on the island to wait on Mr. and Mrs. Maximilian Four were all able to climb up on the small hilly spots that had not sunk into the ocean. Fortunately as well, Gaston, the French chef, had the foresight to bring along a cell phone to call the mainland, and so (hurrah!) every one of them was saved by helicopters sent to rescue them.

But what was un-fortunate was really one terrible thing that really did gang agley. It so happened that on that glorious, sun-swept day, Maximilian P.W.B.T.F. Four and Mrs. Four had decided to take a sun bath on the gleaming white sand of a Rainbow's End beach, and then take a dip together in the sparkling sea, with its gentle waves lapping on the shore.

And that's where they were, holding hands and gazing deeply into each other's eyes, when the island started shivering and shaking and sinking into the sea, taking both of them right along with it.

Rainbow's End had quite simply and finally now turned into the End of the Rainbow. And Maximilian Pettigrew Westmorington Bassford Thorndike Finstersill Smith the Fifth had in one awful, but strangely awesome (like the finale of a movie, if you stopped to think about it) moment, become an orphan.

 # Chapter III

In which Maxilian Pettigrew Westmorington Bassford Thorndike Finstersill smith the fifth learns the dreadful news, and which kicking and screaming and having an oscar-award-winning tantrum could do nothing about.

It was Mr. Fitzbottom, Maximilian Fifth's father's attorney, who came to their penthouse to announce to Maximilian the dreadful news about his mother and father. A lady wearing a white nurse's uniform and a suitably sad expression accompanied him. She wore a badge that said she was Miss Peebly. Mr. Fitzbottom always believed in being prepared for anything that might happen, and he was fully prepared for Maximilian Five to collapse in a heap, or something like it.

Surprisingly, Maximilian did not collapse in a heap, or anything even close to it. He just stood there like a stone statue, with hardly a change of expression on his face. Perhaps he couldn't really believe what he was hearing. Or perhaps he had been alone so much while both parents were off doing such things as buying trinkets for The Golden Truffle, or islands, that being alone was something he was rather used to. The fact that they weren't ever coming back hadn't yet sunk in. Also, it must be said, he had never liked Mr. Fitzbottom very much, and was not going to make a cake of himself collapsing in front of him.

Of course, Mr. Fitzbottom was delighted that he didn't have a hysterical child to deal with. Furthermore, he knew he had a much bigger problem on his hands to deal with and had no idea how he was going to deal with it.

"What's going to happen to me?" Maximilian asked. "Will I just stay here with Mrs. Pinkerpon and Binge and Gridlock and Sir Launcelot and Lady Guinevere and keep on going to Ballyhoo?"

"Not exactly," said Mr. Fitzbottom, giving Miss Peebly a sideways look that indicated he might be more in need of her services than Maximilian.

"Exactly what then?" asked Maximilian.

"I...I...I'm not exactly sure," stammered Mr. Fitzbottom. "We...

we...we'll have to see."

"See what?" asked Maximilian.

"See what's left," said Mr. Fitzbottom.

"Left of my parents?" asked Maximilian. "I thought you said there wasn't anything left of them."

"Of *them*, yes, yes, yes, that's right," said Mr. Fitzbottom. "Nothing left of them, absolutely. It's what else that wasn't left that we must see about."

Maximilian was by now beginning to get a strange sinking feeling in the pit of his stomach. What else not being left has an ominous ring to it? On the other hand, he knew how rich his father was. A lot of his riches could vanish, and there would still be "piles" left. Wouldn't there?

But as it turned out, there wouldn't. At least not that many. By the time Mr. Fitzbottom, relieved at having finished dumping this added terrible piece of news on a disbelieving Maximilian, left with a Miss Peebles, equally relieved at not having to revive a collapsed Maximilian, it had all been explained. And what Maximilian learned was

16

that there were indeed not many "piles" of anything left. The "we'll see" laid on him by Mr. Fitzbottom meant that the "we" was going to see exactly how many and how large. It didn't look very encouraging. On the other hand, nothing was said about no "piles" at all. So there was still hope.

Of course, everyone at Ballyhoo, who knew all about the sad end of Mr. and Mrs. Maximilian Four because it was naturally in all the newspapers, were terribly kind to Maximilian. School was almost out for the summer holidays, but there were enough days left for the school also to learn that there might not be many "piles" left from the Maximilian P.W.B.T.F. Smith the Fourth vast number of them. It wasn't certain, but the Ballyhoo endowment more than likely was among the vanished "piles". Maximilian Five noticed just the tiniest bit of faculty frostiness, and everyone suddenly not treating him as if he were made of spun glass. One teacher actually was quite nasty to him about talking in class.

Pencival was really rather decent at first when he learned what had happened to his friend Maximilian's parents. Hardly anybody likes losing parents, even in such a thrilling way. It could have been himself, after all.

"So what are you going to do now?" he asked. "Are you going to stay in your apartment? Is someone coming to live with you?"

"Probably," said Maximilian, who didn't care to admit that he still had no idea what was to become of him. The "we'll see" part of Mr. Fitzbottom's remarks hadn't yet been revealed to him, which he was afraid didn't bode the best news for his future. But he certainly had no intention of revealing any of this to Pencival.

"Well, bad luck, anyway, old chap," said Pencival, who fancied himself a British school boy in an old British school boy book and had started using expressions like "old chap."

Of course, it didn't take long for word to weave through Ballyhoo that Maximilian's future was on the ropes, so to speak, and there was not only no endowment in sight, there might be no Maximilian in sight either.

At the moment, though, it was mostly guesswork.

Pencival's jolly old chap attitude didn't last long. "I told you I hoped the island wouldn't sink," he said to Maximilian, all but drooling with pleasure. Bathtubs and toilets were beginning to look pretty good to him now. At least *they* wouldn't go "flushing" into any ocean. Ha! Ha!

"Don't worry," said Maximilian, "there's lots more where that island came from." "Lots more" didn't really mean anything. Lots more of what?

It was a good thing Pencival never thought to ask.

At that point, the "we'll see" still hadn't been revealed to Maximilian by Mr. Fitzbottom. Although he was pretty certain a lot of the "piles" were gone, he still felt pretty sure there were quite a few left. How could anyone as rich as his father not have had several spare "piles" left sitting around.

So what if there wasn't one left for the Ballyhoo endowment, or even a "pile" for him to continue going there. There had to be more than just those.

But then things got worse. A whole lot worse when the "we'll see" was finally revealed in its big, mind-numbing entirety. The Ballyhoo endowment and Maximilian no longer being a Ballyhoo boy were just the tip of the iceberg, or the island that held Rainbow's End, if you wanted to put it that way.

For starters, there was no "pile" left to pay for Mrs. Pinkerpon, Binge, or Gridlock. If Maximilian were still to go to Ballyhoo, he would have had to walk. Furthermore, by the time taxes and expenses and everything connected with Rainbow Island were to be paid off, there would not even be the apartment left for Maximilian to live in. Everything in it would have to be sold as well. Even The Golden Truffle would have to go, pink boxes, gold lettering and all. The whole kit and caboodle.

It seemed that Maximilian P.W.B.T.F. Smith the Fourth's plans had really ganged agley in a big,

18

magnificent glorious burst, just like one of the Roman candles that was never to be shot off at Rainbow's End. That it was all due to one tiny sea creature (as was suspected) and one tiny crack on the ocean floor could hardly be believed. But how it happened made no difference in the end.

It might have if there had been insurance to cover it. But as it turned out, that was something else Maximilian Four hadn't actually had the best-laid plans for. It was learned that while he'd fortunately been able to get insurance for all his employees, including Gaston the French chef, only a fifth-rate insurance company would touch what the rest considered a hair-brained idea far too risky to touch with a ten-foot pole, except for a tiny, almost useless amount. You might say it was about as tiny an amount as the crack that finally did in Rainbow's End. The fifth-rate company, faced with such a mountainous loss, promptly declared bankruptcy.

And as it turned up, this was not the entire worst of it for Maximilian Five. It also seemed incredible, but there was no doubt about it that Maximilian Four, should anything happen to him, had no funds, trust or otherwise, set up for Maximilian Five, at least none that anyone could find.

You may remember what Maximilian had told Pencival, that his parents never traveled together, so that if anything ever happened to one of them, the other, complete with fortune still intact, would be left for Maximilian. Who would have known that they would both go down together, not from an airplane flying in the sky, but sinking into the ocean while gazing romantically into each other's eyes?

But does anybody think it can't get worse than this? Please think again.

Because they had arranged for there always to be one parent left for Maximilian if the other one was no longer around, nobody considered the fact that there ought to be some close back-up relative to take him over.

Mr. Fitzbottom probably should have reminded them of this, but somehow never had got around to it. If he had, he would have found there were no relatives at all. This was now sadly discovered when someone actually *had* to think about it.

Maximilian had heard boys at Ballyhoo, including Pencival, talking about cousins and aunts and uncles and especially grandparents who always sent splendid presents for birthdays and Christmas. He had sometimes asked his parents why they had no cousins and aunts and uncles and especially grandparents. There was no reason. They just didn't. Their family tree was only the three of them, and that was that.

It didn't matter all that much to Maximilian. Who needed grandparents, anyway, even if they did give splendid presents? He considered grandparents useless unnecessary wrinkled old people. He didn't like any of them, and said they gave him the creeps. He said that he personally never intended to get old. Besides, he got all the presents he needed without the help of grandparents, thanks to his parents traveling so much and his being able to stage all those super-colossal tantrums.

Of course, *something* had to be done about Maximilian. Just what, Mr. Fitzbottom and "we" had not the remotest idea. It was a particularly knotty problem because he was, they all knew, a snotty, rotten-spoiled kid. Who'd want him anyway?

In the meantime, though, while they were thinking about this, other things had to be done, like selling off The Golden Truffle and the apartment, and everything in both, excluding Maximilian, of course. They held a big estate sale at the apartment to which hundreds of people came. That included Pencival, who arrived with his parents.

"I don't suppose you're going to be able to keep all your toys and games, are you?" he asked Maximilian.

"I don't suppose I am," said Maximilian, which is what he'd been told by Mr. Fitzbottom. There wasn't much use in lying about it now. All those people milling about poking and prodding everything were not there for a tea party.

"That's too bad, old chap," said Pencival, who quite clearly didn't think it was too bad at all. "I'll just look around. My parents will let me have anything I want."

This was probably the lowest blow of all. In the end, bathtubs and toilets had aced Rainbow's End!

When the sale was over, Maximilian had the pleasure of seeing Pencival leaving with an armload of the best games and toys, and a big smirk on his face. Maximilian wandered sadly about from room to room, wondering what his fate would be. If he got down on the floor, kicked his heels, and had the biggest tantrum of his life, what good would it do? Who would care? He was alone in the empty apartment except for Binge.

Mrs. Pinkerpon was gone. Gridlock was gone. Only Binge remained, sitting in the kitchen in his shirtsleeves reading a week-old newspaper, because the newspaper subscription was now gone as well. That evening he would serve Maximilian a frozen dinner or something out of a can.

Maximilian didn't even have Sir Launcelot or Lady Guinevere to talk to, as a home had easily been found for them. They were, after all, valuable purebred Borzois, and snooty, to boot. That seemed to be a quality greatly admired by several people who all wanted them.

"Nobody wants *me*," Maximilian had said to them before they were taken away just before the terrible sale began. "I suppose it's because I'm not purebred."

"Of course you are, dear," said Lady Guinevere.

"Perhaps I'm not snooty and elegant enough," said Maximilian.

"Certainly you are," said Sir Launcelot. "All Ballyhoo boys are snooty and elegant, aren't they? Besides, you can always practice at it. We have, you know."

"I sort of thought you did," said Maximilian. "But there isn't that much time left. Anyway, who wants a rotten spoiled kid."

"Who ran into the street to save a kitten? Let's not forget <u>that</u>! " said Lady Guinevere. "I do hope you will manage to save the gold medal, dear."

"It's already in my pocket," said Maximilian, who had felt like a thief even though he was stealing something from himself. After all, he'd been warned by the people managing the sale that he was *NOT TO TOUCH ANYTHING*!

"You'll write to us, won't you?" said Sir Launcelot. "From wherever you are?"

"I think it might be from an orphanage," said Maximilian, who thought no such thing. He still was all but certain that there was some huge "pile" his father had left for him someplace, and it would soon come to light. But he desperately wanted sympathy, and how better to get it than say you were off to an orphanage?

Maximilian saw the horror in Lady Guinevere's eyes. An orphanage! Oh no!

At any rate, as the telephone hadn't yet been disconnected, Mr. Fitzbottom had called to say he would be coming by late that afternoon with some important news for Maximilian. "Important news" definitely sounded like a "pile" had been discovered. All that remained was to learn how big it was. Maximilian tried to keep "bigness" in mind as he wandered aimlessly through the apartment, though it wasn't easy. His footsteps had a sad, hollow sound as he went from room to empty room.

It was so silent that he nearly jumped out of his skin when the doorbell rang. Binge must have fallen asleep over the newspaper, because it was Maximilian who went the front door.

"Well, my boy," said Mr. Fitzbottom, minus Miss Peebles, but with a toothy smile that reached from ear to ear across his pink, pudgy face and back again, "I believe we have found the answer to our problem!"

 Chapter IV

In which Maximilian five learns enough of his fate, to know that it definitely does not sound too promising, no indeed, not promising at all.

*O*UR problem? Who cared about *OUR* problem, which translated really meant *THEIR* problem.

"What about *MY* problem?" asked Maximilian with a stony face that could crack granite.

"Well...well...well," stammered Mr. Fitzbottom. "*Your* problem then, my boy. It has taken some doing and hours of research, none of which covered by any Maximilian Pettigrew Westmorington Bassford Thorndike Finstersill Smith the Fourth funds, of which I regret to say there are no longer any. All *pro bono*, my lad, entirely. You know what *pro bono* means, don't you?"

Mr. Fitzbottom dropped his face and gave Maximilian a significant look out from under his eyebrows. Maximilian's look back became even stonier. He knew that *pro bono* meant "free". He'd learned that in his Ballyhoo Latin class. But so what? Mr. Fitzbottom must have already helped himself to a big portion (with second helpings!) of a former Maximilian Four "pile". He didn't get that pink, pudgy face from nowhere.

So what could be solved about Maximilian Five's problem if all the elusive (meaning slippery as Jell-O) "piles" were gone. And gone they must be if there wasn't even enough to do some stupid research. Research into what?

"Well," said Mr. Fitzbottom, "we have at last uncovered a relative who has agreed to accept you as *his* problem. What do you think of *that*!?"

"Whoopee!" said Maximilian.

"Now, my boy," said Mr. Fitzbottom, "there's no need to take that tone. You're in a very precarious position, you know. You don't seem to be aware of that."

There stood Maximilian in an apartment so stripped of everything, their voices echoed in the hallway and bounced off the walls of empty rooms. The servants but for one now asleep over an old newspaper in the kitchen, were gone. Maximilian's pets were gone. All his toys were gone. And, of course, there was the small matter of his parents being gone as well. How could Mr. Fitzbottom think Maximilian wasn't aware of all this? Did he think Maximilian was some kind of moron? In answer to the question, he gave Mr. Fitzbottom a look even stonier than the previous two, if that were possible.

"So who's the relative?" he asked. "I didn't know we had any."

"We were beginning to think you didn't," said Mr. Fitzbottom. "It took some fancy sleuthing, I'll tell you, digging into old files and records at the library. As I said, it took hours and hours, and we came close to giving up, but at last we hit the jackpot."

"Jackpot" sounded like money to Maximilian. Maybe things might be looking up after all. "Well, who is he? Or is it a she?" he asked.

"It's a he," said Mr. Fitzbottom. "He's a very distant relative, a fifth cousin twice removed, actually. There must be a million Smith's in this country alone, and it was pure luck that we found the right one. We went out to see the man, and had our findings confirmed by a family tree written up in an old family Bible he had. In it we found that he was related to a Maximilian Pettigrew Westmorington Bassford Thorndike Finstersill Smith the First and Second.

"As there is no doubt not another family in this world with that name, we have to believe this Mr. Smith is also related to Maximilian Pettigrew Westmorington Bassford Thorndike Finstersill Smith the Third, Fourth, and, of course, the Fifth, which is you, my boy. Mr. Marmaduke Smith agrees that this is probably true. And he finally agreed to have you come live with him and be appointed your guardian. Isn't that splendid?"

So far, other than learning that someone had been found who was somehow or other a member of the same family, Maximilian hadn't learned anything splendid about it. If this Mr. Smith "finally" agreed to having him, he must have had to have his arm twisted into doing it. How "splendid" was that?

"What about Mrs. Smith and all the little Smiths?" he asked. "Did they finally agree to have me too?"

"There is no longer a Mrs. Smith," replied Mr. Fitzbottom. "And no little Smiths either."

"What does he do?" asked Maximilian. "Does he own a company or anything like that?"

"Well, let's say he manages a lot of people," said Mr. Fitzbottom. "But, it's a stroke of luck, our finding him, my boy. Furthermore, he's not asking anything for your support, which is also lucky, as, of course, there isn't anything. Our office, has, ahem, taken up a little collection for your bus ticket and a bit of pocket change."

Losing his home and his pets, never mind losing his parents. Pencival, heir to bathtubs and toilets, walking out the house with a smirk on his face and all his best toys. Now Maximilian learned that a collection had had to be taken up for a bus ticket and pocket change!

Rotten spoiled Maximilian, which he definitely was, would like to have done one of two things. He would like to have thrown himself on the floor and had the tantrum of his life. Or, using what he had learned in his boxing class at Ballyhoo, he would have liked to punch Mr. Fitzbottom right in his big fat pink face.

But Maximilian had learned something from Sir Launcelot and Lady Guinevere, who had remained dignified as they were being led away. And after all, he wasn't a Ballyhoo boy and gold medal winner for a heroic kitten rescue for nothing. But most of all, he finally realized there were no "piles" left lying around for him. He was a penniless, parent-less, friend-less, pet-less orphan. He was smart enough to know that the chips were down and he was licked. Mr. Fitzbottom had made his case and won.

So rotten spoiled obnoxious Maximilian took a deep breath and calmly, coolly held out his hand to take the nervous, sweaty, pudgy hand extended to him.

"Thank you, Mr. Fitzbottom," he said.

Chapter V

In which Maximilian finds that if he believes things have finally become as bad as they can get, he is about to learn that no matter how bad things get, they can always manage to get worse.

Maximilian, to date, had managed to keep from shedding any tears. Not even at night in the dark in his room where no one would know about it did tears drizzle down his cheeks. Perhaps because he continued to believe everything was going to turn into a happily-ever-after ending for him. Maximilian had always been a great believer in fairy tale endings. Until he actually got ushered onto the bus by Mr. Fitzbottom, he had continued to believe that there was a "pile" hidden in some bank vault for him somewhere, waiting to be discovered.

But now at long last he had finally and forever given up on this belief. The only "pile" he had was pocket change collected for him in Mr. Fitzbottom's office, two small suitcases that held his clothes, one toy, Mortimer, the shabby teddy bear with one ear half missing (chewed off by Sir Launcelot when he was a puppy) and

Maximilian had slept with since he was two years old, and the gold medal in his pocket.

Finally he now was coming perilously close to having tears happen on the bus ride to the small town located somewhere between nowhere and nowhere, where supposedly a Mr. Marmaduke Smith, who had had to be persuaded to take him in, would be waiting for him.

The one ray of hope left to him was that he considered Marmaduke to be a snooty kind of name. So it was entirely possible that Marmaduke Smith was possessed of some "piles". Looking back on it, Maximilian now realized that Mr. Fitzbottom had avoided giving any details about him other than to say he was probably "about" the age of Maximilian's father. That wasn't much to go on. Furthermore, "about" could mean just about anything. But Maximilian didn't give up easily. He had convinced himself that Mr. Marmaduke Smith was a proud descendant of his own Smith family, and thus could quite possibly be enormously rich.

Binge, who was staying behind to close up the apartment, helped Maximilian pack and get ready for his bus ride, and strongly recommended that he should be dressed comfortably in jeans and a windbreaker. But Maximilian had his own ideas. So he put on his best pair of trousers, his best white shirt, his Ballyhoo blazer with the Ballyhoo gold shield on the pocket, and his blue-and-gold Ballyhoo tie. He had Binge polish up his best black dress shoes. He wanted Mr. Marmaduke and his "piles" to know what he was dealing with when he'd "finally agreed" to take in Maximilian. He wasn't just some piece of driftwood picked up at the beach, or a dirty paper sack swept up on the city street. No indeed!

The bus finally pulled into a small station, and Maximilian struggled down the steps with his two suitcase and five other people. A few people were milling around on the station platform, and he tried to guess which one was going to come up and greet him. When a very nice-looking, well-dressed man about his father's age came toward him, Maximilian put out his hand. But the man went right past him to hug a woman and little girl who had left the bus with him.

A man who had been leaning against a back wall busy reading a ragged paperback book, finally looked up and lifted his faded blue sweatshirt to jam the book inside his belt. Then he began to amble toward Maximilian. The man looked like someone who might have been closer in age to Maximilian Third than Maximilian Fourth so Maximilian Fifth decided at once this could not be Mr. Marmaduke Smith, who was probably late arriving at the station.

Untidy tufts of salt-and-pepper hair poked out from this man's well-worn canvas cap that could have passed for white if not too closely inspected. His baggy blue jeans had a tear on one knee, and his sweatshirt was frayed at the cuffs. The words "Been There, Done That" were also faded, but still visibly printed across the front. On his feet were grimy once-white track shoes.

As he approached closer to Maximilian, Maximilian pretended not to see him. He must be somebody who was going to ask for money. If he wasn't noticed, he might just go away. But the man kept right on ambling until he was standing right in front of Maximilian, practically nose to nose.

"You waiting for me?" he asked.

Maximilian found himself looking into a pair of shrewd, bright blue eyes under bushy salt-and-pepper eyebrows.

"I don't think so," said Maximilian. "I'm waiting for Mr. Marmaduke Smith."

"You're looking at him," said the man. "You must be Max."

"Maximilian Pettigrew Westmorington Bassford Thorndike Finstersill Smith the Fifth," said Maximilian stiffly.

"Whatever," said the man. His eyes were twinkling, but it was a kind of dangerous twinkle. "Do your friends call you that every time they have to say something to you?"

"No, they call me Maximilian," said Maximilian His idea that he should perhaps attempt a Pencival-type sneer departed almost as soon as it arrived.

"Okay, then, Max," said Mr. Marmaduke Smith. "Let's get going." He picked up both Maximilian's suitcases and marched off, leaving Maximilian to scurry after him.

When they arrived at a once-blue station wagon that had clearly seen better days, he threw the suitcases into the rear.

"Climb in, Max," he said.

Max climbed. It was quickly clear to him that arguing with this man wouldn't do him much good. He had been Maximilian all of his life, but for the time being would humor Mr. Smith by being Max. "For the time being" was because in hardly more than an instant, he decided that he would simply have to run away. Run to where he had not the wildest idea. But might an orphanage not be better after all than having to live with this fellow? Running away, though, would take some planning. "For the time being" he would just have to play along.

"Excuse me," he said in his best Ballyhoo boy polite tone, "but how should I address you, sir. Should I call you Cousin Marmaduke?"

"Not if you value your life," replied Mr. Marmaduke Smith. "Just call me Moose."

He began to chuckle. "Marmaduke! My aching eyebrow!"

Every so often as they drove along, he would chuckle again.

Max (as he must now be called) didn't say anything more. He knew that as a "pile"-less, parent-less boy, he didn't have too many choices open to him as to his future in the world. Tantrums were out. So was punching anyone in the nose, especially punching this Moose fellow's nose. This was no flabby Mr. Fitzbottom. It was clear that he was pretty solidly built, and Max had seen him lift two suitcases as if they were filled with feathers. His Ballyhoo boxing class wouldn't help a bit. No, as they drove out of the town and on and on, Max decided the only option was running away.

They drove for some time past houses and several miles of forest. Every so often the road would curve and they could see the ocean. Finally, they pulled into a broad driveway. It curved in front of an enormous, imposing stone house that featured an impressive oak door with stained glass panels on either side. And it was then that a thought suddenly shot through Max like a thunderbolt.

He remembered when once he'd been taken sailing with his father and some of his father's friends on a yacht. The men were all dressed in old, ratty clothes just about like what Cousin Marmaduke, or rather Moose, was wearing. And Max knew they were all enormously wealthy, and dressing that way was just for the fun of it. So if this was the house Moose lived in, he must have a lot of "piles", and could dress any way and even drive any old ratty car he pleased. Max's heart took a sudden leap upward. Maybe he wouldn't have to consider running away after all.

They didn't stop in one of the parking places in front of the fancy door, however, but drove right on past until they arrived at a wide, two-door garage. But instead of going into the garage, they continued past the garage doors to a regular door off to one side, where they finally stopped.

"Okay, this is it," said Moose, starting to climb out of the car.

"This is what?" asked Max.

"Where I live," said Moose. "What did you think?"

"Don't...don't you live in the big house?" stammered Max.

"I hope not," replied Moose. He climbed out and went around to the back of the car.

Max remained frozen in his seat.

"Well, come on," said Moose, dragging out Max's suitcases and setting them down on the ground.

What kind of cousin did Max have who lived in a garage? Was he going to have to start thinking of running away again?

"Who...who *does* live in that house?" asked Max.

"The residents," said Moose. He set down the suitcases and pulled a ring of keys from his jeans pocket. "I couldn't live there if I wanted to. I don't qualify."

"Who...who does?" asked Max.

Moose had put the key in the lock, but didn't turn it. Instead, he just dropped his hands to his side, and gave Max a piercing look. "Your pal, Mr. Fitzbottom didn't tell you?" he said.

"He's not my pal," said Max. "He's a big, fat jerk."

"I see," said Moose. "So what *did* he tell you?'

"Well, when I asked if you were the head of a company, he just said you...you managed a lot of people," replied Max.

Moose grinned. "Well, he's right, in a way. But manage isn't quite the word for it. 'Look after' is more or less what I do."

"Look after who?" Max asked.

"See here, Max," Moose said, "did you read that sign on the highway, and then the brass plate on the front door?"

"Sort of," replied Max,

"And you didn't wonder what they meant?" asked Moose.

"No," said Max. Why would he? He was too busy thinking about either

a) running away or b) figuring if Moose had enough "piles" to make it worth sticking around. Signs and brass plates didn't figure into this.

"Well, the sign and the plaque say Measley Manor," said Moose. "Used to be Dolly Manor, but now under new management. This is a retirement home, taken over by

32

Ruby and Pearl Measley, whom you will be privileged to meet very soon."

"Retirement home?" said Max. "You mean a place where old, wrinkled people live?" Then he added under his breath. "They give me the creeps."

"Sorry to hear that," said Moose. "At any rate, the reason I don't live in that building is because I'm not retired," he went on. "I just work here. I'm the general caretaker, and doer of any odd jobs that need doing. The only reason you're here is because Mr. Fitzbottom explained all that's happened to you, and persuaded me that I'm the court of last resort. So I in turn persuaded the Measley girls we could use extra help right now. Didn't your Mr. Fitzbottom explain all this to you?"

"He's *not* my Mr. Fitzbottom," said Max, gritting his teeth.

"Sorry, I forgot," said Moose.

Of course, the moment Max realized that he was not going to be living in a big stone house with a cousin who had lots of "piles" and dressed the way he did because he *had* to, Max instantly once again decided he would have to run away.

He would walk back to town, and after all, he still had that pocket change collected for him by Mr. Fitzbottom and the rest of the "we" in his office, probably enough for bus fare. He would show up at Mr. Fitzbottom's office and tell them he was ready to go to an orphanage. At least there he wouldn't be around a bunch of old wrinkled people that would give him the creeps, and working for a low-life handyman who probably hadn't even graduated from grade school.

How this man had come to be a member of the Maximilian P.W.B.T.F. Smith family was some kind of freaky accident, or a big mistake altogether. The old Bible that supposedly had this written up had probably been bought by Moose himself at some yard sale.

"Anyway," Moose said, "Come on in to see the place, and you can wipe that scowl off your face. The boys might not like it."

Before Max had a chance to ask another question, or say anything at all, Moose had unlocked the door. As soon as it opened, Moose was instantly attacked on either side by the two boys, both black with assorted white markings.

"Meet Moxie and Mojo," said Moose. "I hope you like dogs, Max."

Now, though Max's mental roller coaster, which had gone plummeting downward in the orphanage-would-be-better-than-this direction, suddenly started slowly back upward in the sticking-it-out direction. But only slowly. Here were two dogs, and Max loved animals. He doubted an orphanage would allow anyone to have animals.

The only thing was that he was used to aristocratic purebreds like Sir Launcelot and Lady Guinevere. They wouldn't have *dreamed* of jumping all over you and covering your hands or face with dog slobber and goo. The running-away roller coaster stalled midway up the incline while Max thought this over.

"Down fellows!" said Moose.

The fellows didn't seem to know the meaning of the word "down" until Moose finally grabbed the two of them by the scruff of their necks and reminded them what it meant.

"So *do* you like dogs, Max?" Moose now made it a question.

"What kind are they?" Max asked.

"Does that determine whether or not you'd like them?" asked Moose. His bright blue eyes were halfway between an amused twinkle and a dangerous challenging twinkle.

"I like all animals," said Max, his chin up. "I...I rescued a kitten from being run over once. I...I won a gold medal for it." He saw no reason to explain that he'd won it from his parents.

"Congratulations!" said Moose, his eyes definitely twinkling. "But in answer to your question, they are the Heinz brothers. The Heinz food company once upon a time had a slogan advertising fifty-seven varieties. So that's what Moxie and Mojo are, just a couple of mutts. Did you have dogs, Max?"

"They were just one variety, Borzois," said Max, who figured Moose wouldn't even know what a Borzoi was.

"You hear that, fellows?" Moose said. "Borzois...Russian wolfhounds. Probably well trained at that. You'd better watch your manners."

Moxie and Mojo just looked up at him adoringly with their tongues hanging out.

"They like walks in the woods. And if an old cemetery a hundred or two years old doesn't creep you out, the fellows like to sniff around the old gravestones." said Moose.

The fellows looked at Moose adoringly and flagged their tails.

Moose gave them both a scratch behind the ears. "So any time you feel like it, you can come on over and take them out."

"Where will I be coming from?" asked Max. "I...I thought I was going to be living here."

"What you see is all there is, and it's barely enough room for me and the boys." Moose replied. "Where you'll be living is the big house."

The big house! So Max would be living there after all, and not in some old room off the garage. The running-away roller coaster was definitely on its way up again.

"I thought you said it was just old people who lived there," said Max.

"I didn't say *just*," replied Moose. "It's where the Measley girls live as well, and I'm taking you to meet them right now."

Girls! If Moose was calling them "girls", might the Measley girls not be nice young ladies who could tell that Max was not just a distant cousin of a handyman living in garage, and there for "extra help" whatever that meant? Besides, it was such a large house, his room didn't have to be anywhere near the old people, did it? It was a very good thing that he had won out over Binge and worn his Ballyhoo jacket. *That* ought to tell the "girls" something. Why, they might even want to adopt him!

After they had managed to escape Moxie and Mojo, jumping on them as they left Moose's quarters, Max picked up one suitcase and went bumping and thumping across the driveway, until Moose snatched it from him and carried them both again as if they were filled with feathers.

They crossed the driveway in silence and arrived at steps leading down a few steps to a cellar door at the back of the building. Moose unlocked the door, but before opening it, he turned to Max.

"Keep your mouth shut as much as possible," he said. "Let me do the talking, and for Pete's sake, Max, don't disagree with anything I say. Okay?"

"Oh, okay," said Max, who had no intention of doing any such thing. He would certainly disagree if he didn't like what Moose had to say.

He was going to let Ruby and Pearl, the Measley girls, know that it was Maximilian Pettigrew Westmorington Bassford Thorndike Finstersill Smith the Fifth, son of Maximilian Etc. Smith the Fourth, and a Ballyhoo boy with a gold medal for bravery in his blazer pocket, they were looking at, and not Max, the poor cousin of the handyman who lived in their garage.

That is EXACTLY what he was going to do!

 # Chapter VI

In which Max is introduced to the Measley girls, and
makes the most of ruining further his already miserable
new life.

Moose then led Max down the cellar hallway toward the stairs.

"My office, if you can call it that," he said, pointing through an open door where Max saw a battered old oak desk covered with piles of papers, a tomato can filled with pens and pencils, and a telephone. Behind it was an old-fashioned oak desk chair, and another like it in front. On the wall was a bulletin board covered with papers tacked untidily to it. Everything looked as if it had been there and used for a very long time, and certainly very different from the office of Maximilian P.W.B.T.F. Fourth, or even the one belonging to Mr. Fitzbottom.

"This is where we hang out when we're working elsewhere in the building," Moose said. "That's the workshop," Moose said, pointing into another room filled with a tools and a worktable. "This is the laundry room, and ahead are the stairs we go up."

"What's in that room?" Max asked, pointed behind him to a door at the end of the passageway that looked as if it were made of steel, and locked with an enormous padlock.

"Not the foggiest," said Moose. "Used to be just a more-or-less empty room collecting dust until the Measley's took over. Then that padlock appeared. I haven't been in it since."

Just before they reached the stairs, there was another closed door with no lock at all, and it was there that Moose finally set down Max's suitcases.

"Aren't we taking those up to my room?" asked Max.

"This *is* your room," said Moose, and opened the door.

Oh no, it isn't! thought Max. Not this room in a cellar with an iron cot and a bed table with a small lamp and no shade on it, a wood chair with one arm missing, a chest of drawers with half its grey paint chipped off and a cracked mirror over it. On the wall were six nails which were the only "closet" the room provided. Moose gave Max a rueful grin. "Sorry about this, kid, but that's the way it is. At least the window's not so high you can't look out and see the trees."

"Bully!" thought Max. Was he supposed to jump up and down and clap his hands because he could see the trees from a dump like this?

"Anyway," said Moose, attempting, but not quite managing, another grin, "you've got your own private bathroom next door."

Considering the look of Max's room, it didn't take any brains to imagine what his "private bathroom next door" was going to look like. No wonder Moose couldn't even produce a grin about it!

But then, Moose suddenly reached into his pocket and pulled out a ring full of keys. He unhooked two of the keys from the ring and held them out to Max.

"Here," he said, "This key's for you to get in the back door. This other one is a key to my place. Any time you want to come over, play a game of ball with the boys, and maybe take them for a walk, they'd love it. I saw how they took to you. Okay?"

Max knew that this was a very special favor. And just because he was where he was, he was still a Ballyhoo boy with manners.

"Thanks!" he said.

But no way, no how, was this going to remain Max's room, or his "private bathroom" either. Big deal that he could look out a window and see the trees! He had every intention of living in some room upstairs where he didn't have to strain his neck looking up to see the leaves, perhaps even a nice loft away from the old people that might remind him of his old penthouse room. But he would keep his mouth shut for now, especially after the kind thing Moose had just done, giving him the key to *his* place.

Anyway, Moose would find out soon enough how things stood with Max and the "girls" at Measley Manor. And after all, Moxie and Mojo were one reason he wasn't making an immediate decision to run away. He'd need the key to go see the boys even if he was in his "penthouse" loft.

When they arrived at the top of the stairs they entered a very large entry hall with wide doors on either side. Through one Max saw tables laid for a meal. Through the other, he saw a television screen flickering, but there was nothing on the screen but snow. Seated in a circle facing the screen were ten chairs. Sitting in each was a very old, very wrinkled person, just the kind that gave Max the creeps. Every grey or white head was nodding, for they were all fast asleep.

"Aw, for Pete's sake! Wait here, Max," Moose said, and stomped across to the television set.

He turned a dial, and immediately a picture returned to the screen. Then he went to a chair and gently shook the shoulder of the occupant.

"Hey, wake up, Mrs. Dumpty, you're missing your program!"

Mrs. Dumpty opened her eyes, gave Moose a big smile. She didn't appear to realize that she'd even been asleep.

Moose then went to the next chair.

"Dr. Humpty, you're missing your favorite program!"

Dr. Humpty opened his eyes, and smiled at Moose. He didn't seem to realize he'd been asleep either.

Moose went from one chair to the other, gently shaking the shoulders of every occupant.

"Hey, open your eyes, Dr. Doodle!"

"Time to wake up, Officer Dickory!"

"You're missing your show, Ms. Bo Peep!"

"Hey, up and at 'em, Mr. Tweedle-Dee!"

"Okay now, open those eyes, Commander King Cole!"

"Didn't realize you've been snoozing, eh, Mrs. Muffet?"

"Hey, you're missing the best part of your favorite program, Coach Winkie!"

"Hi, Mrs. Diddle, you wouldn't want to miss this show, would you?"

All ten were instantly so intent in watching the television set, they didn't even seem to realize that they'd been asleep or that Moose had been there waking them up. He returned to Max shaking his head, with a rueful smile on his face.

Max was wondering meanwhile what all these curious names were, and where he seemed to have heard them before. Then it came to him. They all came out of his *Mother Goose* book, every one! These people must not only be old and wrinkled, but nutty as well, if they answered to these names.

40

"Okay, that's done!" Moose said. "Let's move on."

"Why did you call those people those goofy names?" Max asked. "They aren't their real names are they?"

"Of course not," Moose said. "They put on a little Christmas show for a local kindergarten class a while ago, and acted out *Mother Goose* rhymes. They had so much fun doing it, they decided to adopt *Mother Goose* names. The Dolly's, the former owners of Measley Manor, thought it was fun as well, so the names have stuck. They call themselves the "Mother Goose Gang.""

Max still thought it was loony whatever the reason for it. He didn't think he'd have much to do with these wrinkled old dodo's anyway, though, and the less the better. He didn't even like the idea of living in this house with them should the Measley girls decide to adopt him. This was clearly a very big house, and he'd have to see that his room was as far away from theirs as possible. They had now reached a closed door at the back of the house.

"Brace yourself," Moose said.

"Why?" asked Max.

"Just take my word for it, and do it," Moose said, and knocked on the door.

The door opened slowly, and Max found his eyes glued to two women who could have passed for a pair of steel knitting needles. Their faces featured two identical sharp noses, two identical sharp chins, two pairs of identical sharp, narrow eyes over identical deadly pale cheeks. Their identical black hair was pulled back into identical black buns. The only difference between them was that one wore a large, glittering ruby pin at the neck of her black suit, the other one a deadly black pearl. The Measley girls, Miss Ruby Measley and Miss Pearl Measley, as their pins announced, were a pair of identical twins!

The moment Max saw them, the adoption idea went flying out the nearest Measley Manor window. The two stood for a moment, their narrow eyes studying Max from top to bottom and back up again several times.

"Is this the boy?" asked Ruby.

"He is, Miss Measley," replied Moose.

"Doesn't look like he'll be much use," said Pearl. "Show us your hands, boy."

Moose gave the frozen Max a dig in the ribs. "Show them your hands, please."

"'Please' is not necessary," snapped Ruby. "Do as you're told, boy. Hold out your hands!"

Max held out his shaking hands.

"Not the back, boy, the front," said Pearl.

Max turned his hands over.

"We thought you said he'd done laboring work, Moose. Those don't look like a laborer's hands to us, do they, Ruby?" said Pearl.

"Hmmmph!" snorted Ruby. "Never mind, they will soon enough. I presume you've told the boy what his duties are to be?"

"Not yet," said Moose. "We only just got here."

"Well then, no reason not to let him know now so there's no mistake about it. Don't you agree, Ruby?" said Pearl raising her eyebrows at her twin.

"Oh, absolutely, Pearl," said Ruby. "He's to be helping Snitch until Delilah returns. We presume you also haven't told the boy that Snitch will be in charge. You'll do exactly what Snitch tells you to. Do you get that, boy?"

Max was so paralyzed with fright, he was barely able to nod.

"What you'll be doing, boy, is emptying trash from the rooms and the trash room, cleaning bathrooms, which includes toilets, and possibly helping Mrs. Fiddle in the kitchen. That's to begin with. We'll be considering further duties, of course, but in the meantime, you'll do anything Snitch tells you to do. Anything at all! And see that you do, or Snitch will report it to us. Is that clearly understood, boy?"

Max somehow managed another nod.

"And don't forget, Moose," said Pearl. "The boy is not to be paid anything, as we agreed. Are you getting all this, boy?"

By now, Max's throat so frozen, he was barely able even to breathe, much less manage to nod.

"By the way, Moose, what did you say this boy's name is?" asked Ruby.

"It's..." Moose began.

But before he could get out the name "Max", Max's throat suddenly unfroze just long enough for him to blurt out, "It's...it's Maximilian Pettigrew Westmorington Bassford Thorndike Finstersill Smith the Fifth."

Toilets and trash! Never mind adopting him, there was no way in the world that Max was going to be in charge of toilets and trash, and being ordered about by someone name Snitch. The Measley girls had better know just who it was they were dealing with!

This outburst, however, was followed by a deadly silence. Then the Measley girls turned and looked at one another. Their eyebrows slithered up their foreheads.

"Is there something wrong with this boy, Moose?" asked Pearl.

"No, Miss Measley," replied Moose. "That's actually his name."

"Not any more, it isn't!" snapped Ruby. "He will answer to Max when needed. Is that clear, boy?"

Max nodded again. Oh yes! His big last stand had just collapsed into rubble, and it was very clear indeed!

Pearl's eyes then traveled up and down Max from his polished shoes up past his Ballyhoo jacket.

"Is that all the clothes you have, boy?" she asked.

"N...n...no," stammered Max.

"Well, you can get rid of these," said Pearl. "You won't be needing them here."

But then Ruby dug Pearl in the ribs with a sharp elbow, and motioned her over to a far corner of the room.

There the two of them held a whispered conference, and returned to Max and Moose.

"My sister and I have decided, boy, that you are to keep the jacket and the rest in perfect condition," Pearl said. "We may want you to wear that uniform when we request it. When that time comes, you are to say 'Yes, ma'am, Miss Measley' or 'No, ma'am, Miss Measley' as required. We trust that you will remember this."

Pearl hardly needed to add the words 'or else' to this order. Max was quite able to add them himself!

"You might as well introduce him to the kitchen now, Moose," said Ruby. "And please advise Mrs. Fiddle that's she's late with our tea. This has been a very trying day, has it not, sister?"

"Very trying, indeed!" said Pearl

Then the two Measley girls fixed Max with a stare so sharp that had they really been a pair of steel knitting needles, the points would have gone right through him and come out the other side. They were making it very clear that Max was the reason for their trying day.

As he followed Moose to the Measley Manor kitchen what Max was thinking that with every twist and turn in his life since that terrible announcement made to him by Mr. Fitzbottom, he had been able to think of something that would come along and save him.

But this was it. This was the terrible end. Max's roller coaster had hit rock bottom. He knew now there was but one thing left for him to do. He would absolutely, positively have to run away.

Where he would go and what he would to when he got there, didn't matter. What could be worse than toilets, trash, working under somebody named Snitch, living in a room in the cellar, the cold-blooded Measley girls, a bunch of loony wrinkled old people with stupid *Mother Goose* names, and a handyman who probably hadn't even graduated from kindergarten, much less grade school, even if he had been nice enough to give Max a key to his place to play with the boys.

Anything would better than all that. *Anything!*

Chapter VII

In which Max meets someone else who in all likelihood
will do nothing to improve his future.

Moose led Max across the dining room and through swinging doors into the kitchen. Standing at a large table in the center of the kitchen were two people.

One was a woman in a white apron and pink flowered bandana covering her whole head. She was standing at the table violently chopping a head of cabbage to shreds with a meat cleaver.

Whack! Whack! Whack!

Farther down the table stood a young girl with unruly brown curls dangling over her forehead. She was wearing jeans and a well-worn grey sweatshirt with the words "Mine, Paws Off" printed across the front, and was intent on peeling a potato.

Neither one of them looked up when Moose and Max walked in, at least not until Moose spoke.

"Cabbage stew again tonight, Mrs. Fiddle?" said Moose.

"Of course not, Moose," replied Mrs. Fiddle. "I'm going to wave a chicken leg over it left from two nights ago and call it Chicken Delight. The poor old dears won't know the difference."

"Don't be too sure," said Moose. "But they'll probably be too polite...or *scared* to mention it, all things considered."

"All things considered, indeed!" said Mrs. Fiddle, and down came the cleaver again, whack! "Poor old things! Sad day for them when those lovely Dolly's had to give up this place. Don't know why the Measley girls wanted it, though. Money grubbing old witches! They must think this place is sitting on a pot of gold. Ha!"

Whack! Whack! Whack!

"Wonder why you're still hanging around here, Moose," she said.

"Same reason you are, Betsy. I don't want to leave and let these great senior citizens down. They don't deserve it." Moose said, and then grinned. "Not to mention enjoying the company of the cook."

"Oh, shut up, if you'll pardon me for saying it," said Mrs. Fiddle, turning several shades of pink. Then, without even looking up, she said, "So who's that you have with you?"

"This is Max," replied Moose. "Seems that Snitch has been promoted to Delilah's job temporarily. He'll be Snitch's assistant."

"Snitch's assistant?" said Mrs. Fiddle. "Well, heaven help him!"

"It will only be until Delilah returns," said Moose.

"That is *if* she returns!" said Mrs. Fiddle.

Whack!

"You don't think she will?" asked Moose.

"That's my opinion," said Mrs. Fiddle.

The cleaver came back down, whack!

"Where'd they find him?" asked Mrs. Fiddle.

"They didn't," said Moose. "The kid lost his family, of which I'm some sort of relative, the only one he has that they can find, it turns out. I made the Measley's an offer they couldn't refuse. I told them he'd worked for his

48

father, who was a carpenter and so he was used to hard work. They agreed that he could live here if he helped around the place with no pay. Making it look as if they're doing me a huge favor, of course."

"They would!" said Mrs. Fiddle.

Whack! Whack! Whack!

"Oh," said Moose, "Pardon my manners. Mitzi, this is Max Smith. Max, this is Mitzi Fiddle."

The girl at the table had been busy peeling potatoes while this conversation was taking place, occasionally raising her head to stare at Max with eyes the size of big, blue lamps.

At this introduction, Max just shrugged, while Mitzi made an airy hand wave with the potato peeler in front of her face. Neither one said anything.

"Oops!" said Moose, "I'm supposed to remind you that the ladies are waiting for their tea, Mrs. Fiddle. They say they've had a trying day. I'm just giving you fair warning."

"Hmmmph!" snorted Mrs. Fiddle, "You know what they can do with their trying day!"

However, not wasting a moment, she tore off her apron to reveal a pink shirt and black pants, and her bandana to reveal hair the exact color of Mitzi's although minus the curls. Then she swiftly poured water that had been simmering in a kettle on the stove into a china teapot already sitting on a tray with two dainty gold flowered cups, saucers, napkins, and a plate of tea biscuits.

"Max," said Moose while this was going on, "I've got things to do, so you just stay here and make yourself useful. Why don't you help Mitzi? When you're through, come on back to my place. You might take Moxie and Mojo out for a game of ball if I'm not back. See ya!"

With that he was gone. Moments later, Mrs. Fiddle left, leaving Max and Mitzi alone in the kitchen.

Max just stood there like a post with hands dangling at his side.

Mitzi finally looked at him.

"You want to help me peel potatoes?" she said.

Max shrugged. "I don't know how."

"You mean you've never peeled a potato?' asked Mitzi.

"Never needed to," said Max.

"Well then, take this and watch me," said Mitzi. She opened a drawer under the tabletop, pulled out another peeler, and handed it to Max.

Max couldn't think of any reason not to take it.

"Okay, I can do it," he mumbled, picking up a potato and starting to peel. It really wasn't anything that required brains.

"So I see that you can," said Mitzi. "But how come you've never done it before?"

"I told you," said Max. "I never needed to."

"So who did all the potato peeling in your family?" asked Mitzi. "Your mother or your father?"

"No, our cook," replied Max.

"Did you come from a place like this one?" asked Mitzi.

"No, I just lived with my family," said Max.

"So your family had a cook," said Mitzi. "Whose family has a cook, may I ask?"

"Ours," said Max. "She was Mrs. Pinkerpon."

"Tee hee! Mrs. Pinkerpon the potato peeler!" hummed Mitzi. "And I suppose you had a butler as well?"

"Binge," said Max.

"Binge the butler," hummed Mitzi. "And I suppose your rich family had a chauffeur."

"Gridlock," said Max.

"Gridlock, hmmmm," hummed Mitzi. "That's a great name for a chauffeur. Did he help Mrs. Pinkerpon peel potatoes?"

"No, he just drove our cars. One thing he did was drive me to Ballyhoo, my school, every day," said Max, who couldn't stop himself from bragging. It had become such a habit. But he knew the moment he'd named the school, he shouldn't have.

"Ballyhoo?" Mitzi giggled. "Ballyhoohoo, poopooperdoo. What kind of school has a name like that?"

"Mine," said Max. "It's a private boys' school. *Very* private."

"Oh sure," said Mitzi. "I thought Moose said your father was a carpenter and you worked with him. So how could you be going to a very private boys' school?"

"Moose is lying," said Max. "If you want to know, I'm not just Max Smith, I'm Maximilian Pettigrew Westmorington Bassford Thorndike Finstersill Smith the Fifth."

"So what?" said Mitzi.

"So my father is Maximilian and all the rest the Fourth. You mean you've never heard of him?"

"No," said Mitzi. "Huh! I suppose he's a big fat millionaire."

"Billionaire," said Max.

"Billionaire? Oh wow! So where is this billionaire now?" said Mitzi. "And how come you're here peeling potatoes at Measley Manor?"

"Because the island he bought to have the biggest resort in the whole world called Rainbow's End is mostly at the bottom of the ocean," said Max. "And my father and my mother are down there with it."

Mitzi laid down her potato peeler, and put her hands on her hips. "Well, you know something Maximilian da de whoop de doo, whatever, I think you're the biggest liar that ever lived. I think you're just who Moose says you are. I think your father is a carpenter who might do work for millionaires or billionaires, but that's close as you'll ever come to one. But I'll say this for you, Ballybooboo boy, you do have a great imagination. Won't do you much good around here, though." Mitzi picked her peeler back up and calmly began peeling again.

Whish! Whish! Whish!

"What do I care," said Max. "I don't expect to be around here much longer."

"Where will you be going?" asked Mitzi, giving Max a wicked, sideways grin. "Back to your billionaire pa at the bottom of the ocean?"

"Why should I tell *you*?" said Max.

"No reason," said Mitzi.

They went on peeling in silence. It seemed that the battle lines had been drawn, and Max didn't see any reason to go on with the conversation.

"I guess Moose knows that you'll be leaving," said Mitzi.

Max hesitated. "No, he doesn't yet. And I don't want you to go telling him either. It...it isn't any of your business."

"Don't worry, I won't say anything. Why should I" said Mitzi. "It's nothing to me if you just go or run away."

Max's head snapped around. "Who said anything about running away?"

"Nobody," said Mitzi. "I was just thinking that with your mother and father at the bottom of some ocean, Moose can't very well send you back to them, can he?"

Max went on peeling without answering.

"So," said Mitzi, "Unless you have some other relation who might not mind having a kid dumped on them, there'd be no place for Moose to send you. That means you'd have to stay here, unless you just decided to run away. And if you did, where'd you go?"

"Well, you can just shut up about running away," said Max.

"I'm only thinking," said Mitzi. "And I was thinking if I were to run away, I might end up in an orphanage, and they're terrible places."

"How would you know?" said Max, trying to produce a sneer as good as his former friend Pencival's. "Have you been visiting one recently?"

"No, but I've seen the one in that movie *Oliver Twist*. It's from a book we have to read for a summer school assignment," replied Mitzi. Did you ever see the movie? It's been on TV."

"Sure I've seen it," said Max. "But so what? Orphanages aren't like the ones in that movie anymore."

"You can't be sure about it," said Mitzi. "And suppose a person ended up in an orphanage like that one, they might run away from there as well, and end up picking pockets on the street like Oliver. And if they got caught, ha! They'd end up in jail or someplace not much better. How'd you like that?"

What kind of answer did she expect anyway? Max just shrugged and went on peeling his potato.

"Say," said Mitzi, "how old are you, anyway/"

"Eleven," said Max. "What about it?'

"Nothing about it," replied Mitzi. "I figured that's what you were. So am I. So if you didn't go back to your mother and father at the bottom of the ocean, or run away, and didn't go back to Ballyboohoo, we'd be in the same class at school next year, probably ride the same bus."

"So what," said Max.

"So hurrah!" said Mitzi, producing a bored fake yawn equal to Pencival's best.

"So can I go now," said Max. "I don't see any more potatoes."

"So okay by me," said Mitzi. "I'll let Mum know."

"So thank you," said Max, still remembering Sir Launcelot and Lady Guinevere, and good manners.

"By the way, have you run into Digger and Dork yet?" Mitzi asked.

"Who are they?" asked Max.

Mitzi shrugged. "Oh, just a couple of goons the Measley ladies just hired to work around here," she said.

"What do *they* do?" Max asked.

"Nothing much that I can tell," replied Mitzi. "They mostly just pick a few leaves and pull up a couple of weeds. The Measley's say they're to guard the building, but I think they're here to keep the old people from nosing around. Spying, in other words. That's what Mum says, anyway. Thought I'd warn you in case they catch you leaving here with a suitcase."

Then Mitzi suddenly grinned. "Anyway, good luck with Snitch. You'll absolutely adore him. I guarantee it. See ya" She carelessly waved her potato peeler at Max.

"Not if *I* can help it!" thought Max.

One thing after another, bang, bang, bang, was making it clearer than ever that he had to run away. Toilets and trash. A bunch of old, wrinkled loonies. A pair of twin cold-blooded snakes. A kindergarten graduate handyman. A room in a cellar. And now yet four more horrors had been added to the list, Mitzi Fiddle, Digger and Dork, and probably Snitch, who he was pretty sure from the way Mitzi said it, he would definitely *not* adore. And there was no way that he'd be riding on any bus to school with Mitzi on it, or even going to the same school and being in the same class. No way! No how! Not ever! Not on your life! And he'd have to see about Snitch. If he thought he could order Max around, he'd better think again.

But running away had to be thought through very carefully. Why did Mitzi have go and bring up *Oliver Twist*? Max had forgotten all about that movie. He was ninety-nine percent certain that orphanages weren't like that one anymore. But how could he be sure? What did he really know about orphanages anyway? What about that possible one percent?

Mr. Fitzbottom and his "we" had combed every possible place looking for a relative to dump Max on. There wasn't another one to be had anywhere. Max couldn't even be certain Moose was a relative. Why had Moose even taken him in? Greasing his wheels with the Measley girls. That was probably all he meant to Moose.

If only, thought Max, he had someone to talk this over with, anyone at all. It had to be someone who would care that his parents were at the bottom of the ocean, leaving him not only parentless and homeless, but toy-less and friendless as well (if you considered Pencival an actual friend, that is).

But it had to be someone who would also *not* care that he was now penniless and didn't live in a posh penthouse and have a billionaire father who could leave pots of money to his posh school, and a mother who ran a posh store called The Golden Truffle that also provided delicious truffles useful for bribing friends into being friends.

Then, at last, he finally thought of someone, and he was on his way to see them right now!

Chapter VIII

In which Max gets more doggie slobber and goo, but not much advice regarding loony wrinkled old people, trash and toilets or running away.

T he minute Max opened the door to the Moose's garage apartment, two very excited, happy dogs came galumphing toward him, licking his hands and very nearly knocking him down. Max was delighted.

"Down Moxie! Down Mojo!" he told them.

They paid no attention to the command and went on spreading slobber, goo, and love all over his hands, and his face as well.

"Would you like to go out back and play ball?" Max asked.

"*Yes, yes, yes, yes!*" replied both dogs.

"When we've finished, I'll need your advice," said Max.

"Fine with us, right, Mojo?" said Moxie.

"Absolutely!" replied Mojo. "But let's get going. Please, please, please!"

Max went through the back door with the two dogs charging out ahead of him. There were several old tennis balls strewn across the small yard.

After at least an hour of throw and fetch, Max decided he'd worn them out enough for a drink of water from their tin bowl, a lie down and discussion about his future.

He tried to tell them as best he could something about his past life trying not to do too much bragging. After all, this wasn't Pencival he was talking to.

"*At the bottom of the ocean!*" said Moxie, when Max reached that part of his story. "*That's awful!*"

"How did you stand it?" said Mojo.

"I just did," said Max. "I didn't have much choice. You two look like brothers. You must have lost your parents somehow or other, or else you were just taken away from them. Isn't that right?"

"We have no idea, do we, Moxie?" said Mojo. "We were too young to remember anything. You'll have to ask Moose about it."

"So how did you end up <u>here</u>?" asked Mojo.

Max shook his head gloomily, then gave a deep sigh. "Moose was the only relative anyone could find, and he agreed to take me in. I don't know how Mr. Fitzbottom, my father's lawyer, found him, but I don't believe Moose is a relative even though it says so in a Bible he has. I don't believe it's even his. I think he just agreed to take me so I'd be here to help with the nasty stuff like trash and toilets."

"Oh, I don't know," said Moxie, "Moose is really a pretty nice man. He took us in, anyway, and we're just a couple of mutts who can't help with trash and toilets, or do much of anything useful."

"Where did he take you in from?" Max asked.

"We don't remember," said Mojo. "Like we said, we were too young to remember anything. You'll have to ask Moose about it."

"Anyway," said Moxie, "you said you wanted to ask our advice about something. So what is it?"

Max hesitated, shuffling his feet uncomfortably. "Well," he said, "I'm thinking about running away."

"*Running away!*" both dogs cried at once.

"*You can't do that,*" said Moxie.

"Why not?" said Max.

"Because we like you, and we don't want you to go," said Mojo.

"Don't you really?" asked Max.

"You know we don't!" said Mojo.

The two dogs proved it by jumping up and applying more doggy goo to Max's chin.

"Besides," said Moxie, "where would you run away to? You said Moose was the only relative anyone could find. You don't look old enough to get a job and live by yourself. How old are you, anyway?'

"Eleven," replied Max.

"There you are!" said Moxie. "So I repeat, where would you run away to?"

"I guess I'd go to an orphanage, That's a place where orphans go who have no one who wants them," said Max.

"That sounds pretty grim," said Moxie. Have you ever been to one?"

"No, but I'm sure they're okay," said Max, who was sure of no such thing. "Well, unless they might be like the one in *Oliver Twist*, only I don't think they would be. I don't care what that stupid girl, Mitzi Fiddle, says. Do you know her?"

"Sort of," said Mojo. "She comes around once in a while."

"Anyway," Moxie said, "what if she's not so stupid after all? What if she's right?"

"Hadn't you better think about this some more?" said Mojo. "You might be doing something really, really stupid."

"And who's going to like you better than us?" asked Moxie.

The two dogs jumped up and applied more doggy love to Max's chin.

Before Max had a chance to reply, Moose appeared at the back door, grinning as he saw all the jumping and slobbering going on. As soon as the dogs saw him, they ran over and started leaping all over him as well.

"I see you've all been having a good time, boys, but could I interest you in some supper?" he said. "Like to stay for supper, Max. Generally, I'm sorry to say, you'll just be foraging around in the kitchen for your meals. But how does pizza grab you? Unfortunately, it's a pizza with broccoli. That's our vegetable du jour. You can always pull out the broccoli, if you like. I'll look the other way."

Max loved pizza and oddly enough actually loved broccoli. It was usually just what he ordered. But how did a kindergarten graduate get off using a fancy phrase like "du jour". Who did Moose think he was, anyway? What a moron!

Still, Ballyhoo manners were Ballyhoo manners.

So, "Thanks," said Max.

After the dogs had eaten and Moose and Max had had their pizza watching the news on Moose's small television set, Moose settled down to read.

"You can watch TV, if you want, Max, before you run back to your room," he said. "Won't bother me long as you don't blast my ears off."

But before Max turned on the set, he thought he ought to finish his conversation with Moxie and Mojo. What if he ran away, and nobody cared, and he ended up in a rotten orphanage, or picking pockets on the street and going to jail with no one to come bail him out? He had to know what the dogs thought. When he was certain Moose was deep in his book, Max got down on the floor with the dogs.

"So have you two thought about what I said," he asked in a low voice. "Have you thought about it at all?"

"Sure we have," said Moxie. "And we think you're an idiot."

"Both of you?" asked Max.

"Of course both of us," said Mojo.

"What about trash and toilets," asked Max.

"So what about it?" said Moxie. "Think about what dogs do. You know what I mean, the places dogs sniff and all that. It's where we get our news. So what's so bad about toilets, anyway? Dogs even drink out of them, don't they?"

"I guess so," said Max, who was sure that Sir Launcelot and Lady Guinevere would never do anything as crude as drinking out of toilets. At least he'd never seen them do it. Could it be that they had actually done that and he just never knew it?

"And how about having to wait on all those loony, wrinkled old people who live in that building?" Max went on. "Old people give me the creeps."

"Have you been around lots of old people?" Mojo asked.

Max hesitated. "Not exactly. But I've seen lots of them."

"Seeing and being around aren't exactly the same thing," said Moxie. "Maybe they're not as bad as you think."

"Besides," said Mojo, "maybe later you'll be given something else to do besides toilets, trash, and old people, won't you?" said Mojo.

"But Mrs. Fiddle, the cook, thinks Delilah's not coming back," said Max. "She's the one who's in charge of somebody called Snitch, who does that kind of stuff."

"Thinks she's not coming back, but doesn't know it," said Moxie. "You'd better wait and see, hadn't you?"

"How about that saying, 'Out of the frying pan, into the fire," said Mojo.

"Not to mention we don't want you to go. Please say you won't?" said Moxie.

"*Please! Please! Please!*" both dogs said. Then they put their chins on the floor by Max's feet and looked up at him soulfully.

"I'm only just thinking about it. Okay?" said Max.

Moose looked up from his book. "Is that you talking to the boys?" he asked.

Max shrugged. "Yeah. I was. So what?'

"So nothing," said Moose. "But it almost sounded as if you thought they were talking back to you."

"Well, they were," said Max, and thrust out his chin defiantly. "In case you want to know, I can talk to animals."

"Is that a fact," said Moose. "Hmmm." He returned to reading his book, and that was it.

Max had never had anyone not making fun of him when he said he talked to animals, or call him a liar as Pencival did, or just pretend they believed him the way his parents had, although he knew all along they hadn't and just thought it was "cute". Hadn't he overheard them say this to their friends?

As Moxie and Mojo seemed to drift off to sleep, Max carefully got up to go and turn on the television. But as he stood, he somehow backed into the bookshelf behind him and knocked off a file folder on the bottom row

Some papers slid out of it, and as he started to push them back, the top one caught his eye.

The big, bold print on it was hard not to read even at a quick glance, which was all he got of it before quickly sliding it back into the folder.

Max couldn't believe what he thought he'd seen. It didn't seem possible that Moose could have picked this up at a yard sale like that Bible. The name in fancy print on it was Marmaduke Aloisius Smith. Marmaduke was Moose's real name, so this must have something to do with him.

Max looked over at Moose, deep in his ratty old paperback, and decided he'd better not pull the paper back out of the folder to take a closer look at it. It couldn't be for real, anyway, for if it was, what was Moose doing being a handyman at a place like Measley manner, bowing and scraping in front of those vipers, the Measley girls? He'd have to be some kind of moron to do that. That piece of paper *had* to be a fake.

Still, the fact that Mojo and Moxie were so clearly crazy about him was a lot of points in his favor. This was something Max definitely intended to look into further.

If he didn't run away first, that is!

 Chapter IX

In which Max starts his new job under Snitch, an expert at cleaning pots and pans, among other things, and whom Max definitely does not adore.

After Max returned to his cellar room, he unpacked his suitcases, carefully hanging his Ballyhoo jacket on two nails. He had no idea why the Measley's had wanted him to take good care of it. But then there were a lot of things he couldn't figure out about that crazy place where he'd landed, most of them miserable. His gold medal for rescuing the kitten was still in his jacket pocket, and he decided he might as well leave it there. After all, that medal and his Ballyhoo jacket were the things that meant the most to him.

  After he'd unpacked and put away everything he owned in the beat-up chest of drawers, or hanging on the nails, he finally ventured into his "private bathroom" next door. With unpainted concrete floor and walls, it was as dank and damp and malodorous as Max expected it would be. He spent the least possible time he could there before returning to his room. Too tired to bother with pajamas, he fell into the cot in his underpants.

But once there, with it's lumpy pillow, and only a scratchy old army blanket filled with moth holes to pull over himself, all he did was toss and turn with all the horrors of that day going round and round in his head.

He knew now absolutely he would have to run away, but he also knew it was much easier said than done. And now he'd even found out there were the two "goons", Digger and Dork, guarding Measley Manor. What if they caught him? Running away was going to be difficult enough as it was. Now he had to worry about being caught in the act doing it. Running away was definitely not going to be a walk in the park. And if he ever did do it, it would have to be in the dead of night.

Round and round and round all these grim thoughts spun in Max's head at dizzying speed, before he finally fell into a restless sleep. But it seemed as if he had barely closed his eyes before there was a loud banging on his door. There wasn't even enough light coming through the window so he could see his watch.

But the person banging on the door apparently didn't think it necessary to wait for anyone in the room to issue an invitation to enter. Max heard the person kick the door, which then flew open, banging against the wall behind it. Someone thumped across the floor and turned on his light.

Who, or more accurately, *what* stood there was a boy, probably around sixteen years old. He was of medium height, but thickset, and with a face that more closely resembled a flat, pie tin than anything else. His hair of some nondescript pale color, was clipped short and stood out from his head like the quills of a porcupine. Over thick lips, and a nose flat spread out as if the owner might have once fallen on it and it never returned to any reasonable size, were topped by pale blue eyes the color of dishwater.

"Okay, you little turd," said this apparition, "you might's well get it into your swelled head that you ain't on bankers' hours no more. You got to get up now 'cause you got work to do. And no use puttin' on any o' your high an' mighty airs an' fancy names. Mz. Measley tol' me all 'bout that. Long as Delilah ain't here, I'm boss, and you're workin' under me. You got that?"

Max, barely awake, was too stunned to do any more than nod.

"My name is Snitch, like you been told," said the boy, but I'll be expectin' you to call me Mr. Snitch. You got that?"

"Y...y...yes," stammered Max.

"Yes, what?" snapped Snitch.

"Yes...Mr....Mr. Snitch," replied Max.

"That's more like it, you little turd," said Snitch. "Now, I expect you'll be needin' to go to the terlit, so I'll wait here for you. And be quick 'bout it."

Max did not need a second advisory. He quickly climbed out of his cot, and grabbed the jeans and shirt he had hung on the nails not holding his jacket and dress trousers. Nasty as the "terlit" was, he had no intention of dressing under the watchful eye of Mr. Snitch.

Nor did he have any interest in staying any longer than was necessary in that miserable washroom. He was back in his room in no more than few minutes. But that was long enough for Snitch to have taken his jacket off the nails it hung on, and was trying to shove his bulging shoulders into it.

"You get that off!" Max shouted, not even taking time to think.

"Get that off, what, you little snot?" Snitch shot back, still trying to shove his arms into a jacket that there was no way in the world he could actually fit into.

"Get that off, Mr. Snitch!" said Max.

"Who says so?" said Snitch.

"Miss Ruby and Miss Pearl say so," said Max. "They told me to keep the jacket looking nice."

"What for?" said Snitch, suddenly hesitating before trying to shove any further.

"I don't know," said Max. "They didn't say."

"I think you're lyin'," said Snitch.

"Then ask them and see," said Max.

Snitch shrugged. "I'll just do that, you little weasel." He pulled the only arm out from the jacket that he'd been able to squeeze into, and slammed the jacket onto the nails. Unfortunately, out from the pocket fell Max's gold medal.

Snitch lost no time in snatching it up. "What's this?"

"A medal I won...I won it at...school for...for boxing," said Max, who had not been trading lies with Pencival for years for nothing. He had become an expert at it.

"Huh!" snorted Snitch. "If it's for boxin', what's a cat doin' on one side?"

"That's not a cat," said Max. "It's...it's a tiger."

"How come a little weasel like you got a medal for boxin'?" said Snitch. "You musta been boxin' a midget."

"That's all you know," said Max. "Anyway, you'd better put it back in the pocket. The...the Measley's wouldn't like you taking it."

"They know 'bout it?" asked Snitch.

"Sure they do," said Max. After all if you've lied about one thing, no reason not to lie about it all.

"Aw, who wants it anyway? Probably made o' tin," said Snitch, and shoved the medal back into the jacket pocket.

"It happens to be gold, for your information," said Max, and then instantly regretted saying it when he saw the sly look come over Snitch's face.

"Well, la da *da*," said Snitch. "Maybe it is and maybe it ain't. But you ain't gettin' gold medals for what you're gonna be doin' now. You got that, you little dirt bag?"

"Yes," said Max

"Yes, what?" said Snitch.

"Yes, Mr. Snitch," said Max.

"That's more like it," said Snitch. He picked up a bucket filled with bottles, rags, and brushes he'd parked outside Max's door, and handed it to Max. "You take this and follow me. We start off in the kitchen cleanin' up from last night's meal."

Marching up the cellar hall, he clumped up the stairs, with Max stumbling along with the bucket behind him.

When they reached the kitchen, they were greeted with a pile of dirty pans and bowls heaped in the sink. There were stacks of dishes on the counter, as well, but they at least looked if they had been rinsed.

"All right, you little toad," said Snitch, "Now I'll just make myself a cup o' tea 'n' sugar, and some buttered toast n' jelly for me breakfast, and watch to see if you know what cleanin' up dirty pans and dishes is all about."

So sitting with his big boots up on the kitchen table, Snitch did exactly that, all the while advising Max on how to scrape and scrub just about every pot and pan and bowl and dish he picked up. Max could have figured it all out by himself. He'd hung around Mrs. Pinkerpon in their penthouse kitchen enough times that he hardly needed instructions. But Snitch apparently saw no reason not to offer them anyway.

When Max, his hands raw and red, finally finished the last pan, he said,

"Am I going to get anything to eat?"

"Anything to eat, what? You talkin' to me?" said Snitch.

"Am I going to get anything to eat, Mr. Snitch?" said Max.

"Same thing as me," said Snitch. "I left you a piece of toast, and I guess you must o' learned how to pour y'r own tea, and don't need no lesson from me. But be quick 'bout it. We got to start takin' out the garbage and start in on the rooms."

The piece of toast Max had was by then stone cold, without any benefit of the butter or jelly liberally applied to Snitch's three pieces, and the tea was just as cold and, of course, with no sugar. And while Max stuffed down this sumptuous feast, Snitch stood at the door tapping his foot to let Max know he was using up valuable time.

"Now we start in the rooms, partikerlarly the bathrooms," said Snitch, once he had supervised Max lugging three sacks of garbage out the back door and dumping them into the garbage bin. This, of course, was done with benefit of Snitch issuing instructions on *exactly* how garbage should be dumped.

Just as Max was dumping the last load, he saw a truck driving up, and

two men climb out. They were both wearing dark blue overalls and with some kind of badges on their chests.

"Watchdogs arrivin', I see," said Snitch. "That's Digger 'n' Dork, lest you ain't been told yet. You better steer clear o' them if you know what's good for you."

This coming from Snitch almost made Max laugh. In his opinion, it was Snitch himself he'd like to steer clear of.

Then, as they were leaving the kitchen, Mrs. Fiddle and Mitzi arrived.

"Got it all cleaned up like usual, Mrs. Fiddle," said Snitch.

"Thank you, Snitch," replied Mrs. Fiddle. "Did Max help you out?"

"Oh, yes, he did a little," said Snitch. "He got a lot to learn 'bout cleanin' though. But not to worry. I'll be teachin' him."

Mitzi just grinned as she brushed by Max. "Told you so," she said. "Have fun Ballybooboo boy!"

Max at that moment wasn't sure which one he hated most, Snitch or snotty Mitzi Fiddle. Well, they might just as well know, he was *not* going to stick around Measley Manor long enough to find out.

Chapter X

In which Max is introduced by Mr. Snitch into the fine art of bathroom cleaning, which includes sinks and tubs and "terlits," and meets an actual old person.

"**N**ow, this here's Mrs. Dumpty's room," Snitch said. "I'm guessin' Moose told you 'bout their crazy names. But don't you go talkin' 'bout them gold medals an' fancy jackets. It's none o' their business, and they're not interested anyhow. So you just keep your trap shut. You got that?"

"Yes," said Max.

"Yes, what, you dumbbell?" said Snitch.

"Yes, Mr. Snitch," said Max.

"An' don't you forget it," said Snitch, and knocked on Mrs. Dumpty's door.

"Who is it?" a sweet voice called out.

"It's y'r cleanin' crew, Mrs. Dumpty," said Snitch in a voice quite different from the one he used on Max.

"Come right on in," sang out Mrs. Dumpty.

Snitch entered, with Max and his bucket trailing behind.

Seated on a big armchair in the corner he saw a little lady dressed in a pink shirt, slacks and stocking feet.

"Where's Delilah," asked Mrs. Dumpty.

"Oh, she's off havin' to see some relations," said Snitch. "I'm in charge whilst she's gone," he added, his chest visibly swelling.

"And who is this young man with you?" asked Mrs. Dumpty.

"He's to be my helper," said Snitch. "Don't know a thing 'bout cleanin',

but I'll be learnin' him what's what. Never you fear."

"Does he have a name? asked Mrs. Dumpty.

"It's Max," said Snitch, which was the first time he had called him anything but a little turd and other such names. Max had been beginning to think Snitch didn't even know his right name.

But he decided against giving his full name the way he'd done with the Measley's. What was the use? He didn't need to prove anything to Mrs. Dumpty, and Snitch would only take it out on him later, making his life even more miserable.

"Well, how do you do, Max," said Mrs. Dumpty.

But while it was true you could take a boy out of Ballyhoo, you could never take Ballyhoo out of a boy. Almost without thinking, Max went up to Mrs. Dumpty with his hand outstretched.

"How do you do, Mrs. Dumpty," he said, bowing slightly, as she reached out her hand to shake his.

Mrs. Dumpty's eyes widened. It was clear that this startled her. She gave Max a searching look, but she said nothing about it, and simply gave him a warm smile.

"Well, I'm afraid, Snitch, there's not much Max can learn today. My bathroom is quite clean, I assure you," said Mrs. Dumpty.

"Never mind," said Snitch. "I been ordered to do the bathrooms, clean or not. Besides, like I said, I got to learn

Max a thing or two 'bout the cleanin' business. So if it's alright with you, we'll just go in and get started."

The minute they entered the bathroom, Snitch said, "Well, Max, main thing I'm goin' to learn you 'bout is the terlit. Now watch me careful. You see that first thing you got to do is lift up the lid, like this."

This was said in such a loud, important voice that there was no doubt it was intended for Mrs. Dumpty to hear.

"Now, Max, you got that?"

"Yes, Mr. Snitch," said Max dutifully. He wondered if Mrs. Dumpty thought he'd gone all his life without knowing about lifting toilet lids. Still, she was only a wrinkled old person, so what did it matter?

"Now," said Snitch. "What you do is take that bottle with the green sticker on it from y'r bucket. You screw off the top, and then pour some right into the terlit. So let's see you do it."

Max unscrewed and poured.

"Okay, then," said Snitch. "Now you take the brush what's sittin' behind the terlit, and you go swishin' 'round inside."

Max swished.

Snitch peered down into the now spotless toilet.

"You missed a spot," said Snitch, in an even louder voice. "Now go 'round swishin' again. You got to get every spot."

Max went around again.

Snitch stuck his nose into the toilet.

"Well," he grunted, "It's y'r first time doin' it. Next time you can do better. So put down the lid, and we'll do the shower floor."

Max by now knew there was no "we" about it. Snitch was going to do the ordering, while Max did all the working. But as Max lowered the toilet lid, he saw something that had been hidden when Snitch raised it, which instantly erased all thoughts of Snitch from his mind. What he saw was the name of the company imprinted on the back of the bowl. It was the name of Pencival's father's company! Of all the terrible things that had happened to Max, this came very close to being the worst. He could see Pencival laughing his head off over it.

Max's brain was so filled with this depressing sight, that he never even felt the pain in his knees as he scrubbed the shower floor, or cared that Snitch made him do it all over again twice after the first time.

Then, as he and Snitch were preparing to leave the room, Mrs. Dumpty called out. "Snitch, I'd like to ask your assistant to help me with my shoes. Could you wait in the hall for him for just a moment?"

"Er...well, all right, Mrs. Dumpty," said Snitch, so taken off guard, his brain couldn't come up quickly enough with a reason why Max couldn't do as requested.

But he managed to hiss at Max before he walked out the door, "You do what Mrs. Dumpty wants, but be quick 'bout it, you little weasel."

Snitch, of course, left the door open so he could get a full view of what was going on,

"Darlin'" said Mrs. Dumpty, "Something Delilah always helped me with was putting on my shoes. Hope you don't mind doing it for me, please. My shoes are right here beside me."

Max actually minded very much. What he'd learned in the bathroom was bad enough, but putting shoes on the feet of a wrinkled old person was about more than he could bear. On the other hand, he was still a Ballyhoo boy with manners, and wouldn't telling Mrs. Dumpty that putting on her shoes wasn't in his job description be bad manners? He quickly picked up the shoes and kneeled down in front of her. If things weren't bad enough, here was having to put shoes on the skinny, boney feet of a wrinkled old person that would usually give him the creeps.

As he was doing this, she whispered, "Here take this," and thrust a small folded note into his hand. "Put it in your pocket, darlin', and read it when you're alone sometime."

Then she raised her voice and said, "Snitch," she called out, "thank you for letting your assistant do this for me."

"Oh, no problem, Mrs. Dumpty," replied Snitch grandly. "Any ol' time."

But the minute the door closed behind them, he hissed at Max, "So what was she whisperin' to you 'bout, you little turd?'

"Nothing," said Max. "She just said thank you."

"Well, all right, then," said Snitch. "Just no more whisperin'. You got that?"

"I got it, Mr. Snitch," said Max.

Then he sneaked the note from Mrs. Dumpty into his jeans pocket.

But by the time he had been instructed in the fine art of bathroom cleaning in the rooms of all the other residents, Max had forgotten all about Mrs. Dumpty's note.

Chapter XI

In which Max finds out something about all the mother goose-ites, and a few lessons in the course of "old people 101."

Later, by the time Snitch had repeated the exact same bathroom routine in every one of the *Mother Goose-ite* rooms, Max felt he could write a book on the subject. Of course, his hands were so red and sore, he wouldn't have been able to work a computer, a typewriter, or even hold a pencil.

But one thing he learned was that there were indeed some very interesting old people living in Measley Manor.

"Avast and belay," shouted Commander King Cole when Snitch knocked on his door. "Enter and identify yourself."

Snitch and Max entered a room that had a big brass anchor hanging on the wall surrounded by pictures of navy ships.

"This here's Max," said Snitch. "I'm in charge while Delilah's away, and he's my helper. I'm learnin' him the cleanin' business, you might say."

A man with a great mane of white hair, wearing a sweatshirt about like the one Max was wearing, jumped up from a chair at a desk.

"Splendid! You'll find it all shipshape, but clean away, if it pleases you."

Then when the cleaning job had been done, the man jumped up again, and this time, stiff as a ramrod, gave them a smart salute.

Now it so happened that Max had not only practiced sneering in front of a mirror so he could out-sneer Pencival, but after a sail on his father's yacht where all his father's friends were having a good time saluting each other, Max had practiced saluting as well. Now he finally had a chance to properly salute, and a real sailor as well, so he stood up straight as he could, bearing in mind that he was holding a heavy bucket in one hand, and smartly saluted Commander King Cole.

Commander King Cole beamed. "Splendid, my lad! Splendid!"

Of course, Snitch didn't think it was splendid at all. The minute the door closed behind them, he gave Max a painful pinch on the arm he'd used for saluting. "Don't you never do that again!" he hissed. "Tryin' to make me look bad. You do it and I'll see you'll be wearin' that arm in a sling, you little turd. You got that?'

"Yes, Mr. Snitch," said Max, who could barely lift his arm anyway by now. The salute had actually been painful.

But so far, at least, Max had met two old people, and neither one had given him the creeps. Still, there were eight more to go.

"See you don't do nothing stupid with the others," said Snitch, applying another pinch to Max's arm.

"Yes, Mr. Snitch," said Max dutifully. He had no intention of risking yet another pinch from Snitch's thick fingers.

"This here lady was oncet a detective," said Snitch as he knocked on the door of Miz Bo Peep. "So you better keep your weaselly mouth shut 'round her, and don't go talkin' about your fancy jacket and gold medals. She'll think you're lyin' anyhow."

"Enter!" a voice called out.

The voice sounded old and crackly, so Max expected to see someone all huddled in a chair with a shawl around her shoulders. She was an old person, all right, but was dressed in a neat navy-blue pantsuit and was standing at a table with an enormous magnifying glass in her hand. On the table lay a large sheet of paper with what looked like rows of fingerprints on it.

"Don't tell me, Snitch," she said. "Let me guess. Delilah's away and this young man is helping you out with your duties. Is that right?"

"You guessed right, Miz Bo Peep," said Snitch. "I'm learnin' him the cleanin' business. He ain't much good at it, but I'm tryin' hard."

"I'm sure you are," said Miz Bo Peep, who like Mrs. Dumpty, gave Max a long hard look, but kept quiet about what she had learned from it.

"Well, learn him away then, while I get back to work," was all she said.

The man who came to let them in at the next room was wearing a white sweat suit with a pair of red satin shorts over it. He had a basketball in his hands. This was Coach Winkie, and after Snitch gave his familiar speech about "learnin' Max the bathroom-cleaning business", and was issuing orders to Max in the bathroom, they could hear the ball bouncing into a basketball net hanging over the front door.

But as they were leaving, Coach Winkie suddenly said to Max. "You ever played basketball in school, young man?"

Now, having been ordered by Snitch to keep his trap shut, Max just shrugged.

Then, without any warning, Coach Winkie said, "Catch!" and threw the ball at Max. Max instinctively caught the ball, twisted, and lobbed it right through the hoop, catching it as it fell.

"Thought so," said Coach Winkie. "Couldn't get Snitch to do that. He's pretty good, don't you think so, Snitch?"

Max could see from the look on Snitch's face that what he was thinking wasn't printable. Oh, how he wished he'd missed that basket

"You'll have return and have a game with me, young man," said Coach Winkie.

Max just shrugged and didn't bother with a Ballyhoo "thank you".

He knew what was waiting for him with Snitch the minute the door closed behind them! And, naturally, he wasn't wrong. Calling him a little turd who was just showing off, and better not try it again if he knew what was good for him, was only the beginning of it. Max began wondering if he'd ever make it until the end of the day. He could only hope he'd remain invisible to the rest of the old people. That seemed impossible, though, as long as Snitch continued to brag about "learnin' him" the bathroom cleaning business!

The next room belonged to Officer Dickory.

Officer of what Max discovered as soon as they entered the room. Although he was wearing the same kind of sweat suit as Coach Winkie, pictures lined up the wall were of Officer Dickory in a police officer's uniform. In some of the pictures he was by himself, but mostly he was with important looking men, or having a medal pinned on his chest.

After their bathroom business was done, Max was breathing a sigh of relief as they were ready to leave the room. He hadn't been noticed by Officer Dickory, and would not have to suffer another lecture from Snitch as soon as the door closed behind them.

And then Officer Dickory called out, "Just a moment, young man, come on over and let's see how clever you are at picking out a criminal among these pictures."

Snitch dug him in the ribs. "Well, go on, do it!"

So Max went over to the pictures, and picked out the most unlikely person he could.

Officer Dickory chuckled. "He's actually the president of a bank and a splendid fellow. Criminals don't always look like criminals, you know, my boy. Why, Snitch picked the right one out right away. But come again, young man, and we'll have a lesson in how to...er...finger a criminal."

"See, you ain't so smart, you little weasel," said Snitch.. "Don't know a thing 'bout fingerin' criminals like me. But you better not go back 'lest I'm with you. And no talkin' 'bout that stupid gold medal neither."

"Yes, Mr. Snitch," said Max, grateful that he'd escaped that room as easily as he had. It was a good thing he'd thought fast enough to pick a bank president as a criminal!

After that cleaning job, they made trip to the kitchen to pick up what food Mrs. Fiddle had for them left over from the last night's dinner. Although Max didn't care if he never saw Mitzi again, she was unfortunately there with her mother, and grinned when she saw him.

"Having fun, Ballybooboo boy?" she said under her breath when they passed each other. "What kind of toys you got in that bucket? Show them to me, huh?

Max just shrugged and didn't bother to reply. What was the point of any conversation with a girl like that? She wasn't even worth arguing with. The less he saw of Mitzi Fiddle the better.

After their meal, back they went to Max's bathroom-cleaning lessons. Except for one slip-up, he was grateful that he escaped each room without the usual Snitch lecture or painful pinch on the arm.

The one slip up was when they went into Mrs. Doodle's room. Mrs. Doodle turned out to be Dr. Doodle, a veterinarian, who asked Max if he'd ever had any pets. And Max stupidly lost his head, and said, "Two Borzois."

"Ah yes, Russian wolfhounds," said Dr. Doodle. "Very elegant, aristocratic, and I might add expensive dogs. Were they actually yours?"

"Yes, they belonged to my family," said Max.

"Ah, I see," said Dr. Doodle.

"Bor-wotevers! Gold medals! Wot you had was mutts and a piece o' tin," said Snitch, the moment they were alone together. "And y'r nothin' but a lyin' little snot!"

"Guess so, Mr. Snitch," said Max, who was almost ready to believe it. In just a few days, he had almost forgotten that he had ever had another life.

And it looked as if even with the few nice people he'd met, Moose, who he was beginning think wasn't all that bad, and the surprising old people, plus Moxie and Mojo, the rest of his grim life was going to go on forever. Unless he did something about it, which he still might. Yes, he absolutely still might! The running-away roller coaster hadn't hit rock bottom yet, but it was close. And it would take planning so he wouldn't make some stupid mistake if and when the roller coaster ever got there.

After Dr. Doodle, Max met and then continued his bathroom-cleaning lessons under Snitch in the room of Mrs. Muffet, also *Dr.* Muffet, who with her once husband, had been an anthropologist and had the most wonderful cabinet full of assorted bones, flint arrowheads, shark's teeth and all sorts of interesting objects. When she asked Max if he'd like to have a closer look at it all, he would love to have said "yes!" But one look at Snitch's face, and all he did was grunt like an idiot.

Dr. Humpty was a "perfessor o' astronomy" announced Snitch proudly, as if he had invented the subject, when he introduced Max. But when Dr. Humpty invited Max to have a look through the enormous telescope at his window, Snitch gave him such a warning look that he just stood and shook his head like a moron while Snitch explained that they "ain't got time for that today."

Mrs. Diddle arrived to open her door with a paintbrush in hand and wearing a billowing yellow smock streaked with paint. An easel by her window showed that she was half finished painting the scene outside her window. Max could see that many of her paintings hanging on the wall were of the same scene outside her window, done over and over again as if she hadn't left the room in a long time. But other paintings were not, and even had blue first prize ribbons attached to the frames. Max would love to have taken a closer look at all of Mrs. Diddle's beautiful paintings, but he knew what the answer would be to that if he asked Snitch. So he just looked into Mrs. Diddles' "terlit" and shower floor instead.

The last room they went to belonged to Mr. Tweedle-dee, a former animal trainer who, despite Snitch's scowling face, managed to ask Max if he knew Moose's dogs, Moxie and Mojo.

"I was able to give them a few training lessons before the Measley's took over Dolly Manor, and I was informed I could no longer leave the building to do it," said Mr. Tweedle-dee.

But before Max could tell him about the jumping up and the slobber and goo which might need further reminders from Mr. Tweedle-dee, he had already been dragged off for his own reminders about "terlits" and shower floors from Snitch.

By the time Snitch had left for the day, and Max had collapsed in his cot with sore hands and aching knees, he realized something. He suddenly realized that his former ideas of old wrinkled people had changed remarkably. He no longer hated them. They could be very interesting. And most important of all, they no longer gave him the creeps.

On the other hand, so what? That didn't change much else in his life. He was still living in a room in a cellar and under the iron fist of "Mr." Snitch, He would miss Moose whom he sort of kind of liked (though it was hard for him to admit it) and definitely Moxie and Mojo if he left, but that was all.

All things considered, although the running away roller coast hadn't quite reached rock bottom yet, it was still perilously close to getting there.

Chapter XII

In which Max manages to survive an encounter with the Measley's, makes a ridiculous promise, learns why he was told to keep his ballyhoo jacket looking nice, and then finally makes a miserable discovery.

"**W**hat may we ask are you doing prowling the halls?" said a menacing voice.

"Have you no chores to do?" said a second, equally menacing.

"S...s...Snitch and I have finished and he's gone home," stammered Max. "I...I...was on my way to...to the kitchen to see if I could help Mrs. Fiddle." That, of course, was only partly the truth. He was actually starving and even though it might mean running into Mitzi, he hoped to find something like a piece of bread or just about anything to eat.

"Ah, splendid!" said Ruby Measley, for one of the voices was indeed hers. "It seems we were right in allowing Moose to bring this boy here, and from the generosity of our hearts, I might add. Don't you agree, Pearl, dear?"

"And finding him here is very convenient just at this time, wouldn't you say, Ruby," said Pearl, who turned to her sister with one eyebrow slithering up her forehead.

"Oh yes, *very*," replied Ruby, with an eyebrow likewise slithering upwards. "You see, dear boy, we were coming anyway to tell you to wear your nice jacket and meet with us in the lobby. But we want you to know that my sister and I could see when we first met you though we might not have shown it, that we think you are a very clever young man."

"Yes," said Pearl, "A clever young man who knows which side his bread is buttered on."

"Who wouldn't turn down a main chance when it's offered to him," said Ruby.

"Who knows a good thing when he sees it," said Pearl.

"Who wouldn't look a gift horse in the mouth," said Ruby.

"Who wouldn't put all his eggs in one basket," said Pearl.

"I don't believe that one quite fits, Pearl, dear," said Ruby.

"Oh, that's okay," said Max, "I...I think I get the picture."

"Of course you do, dear boy," said Ruby. " And that being the case, we would like to propose something to you, besides wearing your jacket, that is."

"Yes," said Pearl. "You see we have reason not to trust any of the old birds."

Ruby cleared her throat.

"I mean the dear old souls," said Pearl. "We don't know what they might be up to, you might say."

Max hesitated. "What...what could they be up to?"

"We have no idea," said Ruby.

"Which is where you come in," said Pearl.

"We'd like you to keep an eye out for us," said Ruby. "You know, just let us know if anything unusual is going on that we should know about or if anyone finds some...er...curious old papers like maps that really belong to us."

"And report it to us," said Pearl.

"You mean spy?" asked Max.

"Oh, that's such an unpleasant word," said Ruby, with a deep sigh. "But if you must put it that way."

"You would certainly be rewarded for any information you bring us," said Ruby.

"Do you like chocolates?" asked Pearl. "Would you like a nice big box of chocolates? That's what Mitzi said she'd like."

"Did...did Mitzi say she'd spy for you?" asked Max. Well, he might have known she would! It didn't surprise him a bit.

"Oh yes," said Pearl. "She...er...is a very clever girl who knows which side her bread is buttered on."

"Etcetera," added Ruby.

"Well," said Max. "Chocolates make me break out in spots. "I've never been able to eat chocolate." This, of course, was a major lie. He had, after all, devoured boxes of chocolate truffles from The Golden Truffle.

"So how would you like to be rewarded?" asked Pearl.

"How about money?" said Max.

Ruby and Pearl exchanged raised eyebrow glances. "Well, perhaps that could be arranged," said Ruby.

"And do we take this to mean you'll do it?" asked Pearl.

"Spy you mean?" asked Max.

Both Measley girls nodded, all smiles.

"Oh sure," said Max, "Why not?"

"Splendid," said Ruby, with a triumphant smile to her sister.

"Now go change into your trousers and put on your jacket, and meet us in the lobby," said Pearl.

"And remember," said Ruby, suddenly losing the friendly smile and, looking at Max with narrowed eyes, "whatever is said, you are only to say 'yes, ma'am, Miss

Measley' or 'no, ma'am, Miss Measley'. Is that quite clear?"

"Yes, ma'am, Miss Measley," said Max.

"Splendid!" said Pearl. "He'll do nicely, Ruby. Now run along and change, boy."

Max ran. He would like to have run right out of Measley Manor if he could get by those two goons out there patrolling, but instead, he raced down to his room. When he arrived in the lobby in trousers and Ballyhoo jacket, he learned what this was all about.

In the lobby were a man and woman and with them an old lady. And standing before them were two women it took Max several moments to recognize as the Measley's. How they had managed such a transformation in such a short time, he could not imagine. But both had changed their hair styles, applied make-up that made them look twenty years younger, and changed into handsome pant suits with frilly pink blouses cascading down the front.

"Why here is young Maximilian," said Ruby, patting Max on the head. "He attends a near-bye private school as you can see from his jacket. He is the grandson of one of our residents and comes often to do volunteer work. Isn't that so, Maximilian, dear?"

"Yes, ma'am, Miss Measley," lied Max.

"Why," added Pearl, "Maximilian only recently helped in one of the many activities we have for our residents when they put on a lovely performance doing stories from *Mother Goose* for the dear little children from our local elementary school. Isn't that right, Maximilian?"

"Yes, ma'am, Miss Measley," lied Max.

"And, of course," continued Ruby, "he often joins with them when they come together to watch their favorite television program. We always see that they are served tea and cakes from our splendid dining room where only the most delicious meals are served. Isn't that true, Maximilian?'

"Yes, ma'am, Miss Measley," lied Max.

"Well, you may run along now, dear boy," said Pearl. "We are going to show Mr. and Mrs. Kelly and their grandmother Mrs. Kelly a sample of the lovely room she might be occupying."

Max knew exactly the room Grandmother Kelly would be shown. Snitch had shown it to him several days earlier and pointed it out as the "Show-off Room," a room that bore no resemblance to the shabby rooms occupied by everyone else.

He could hardly wait to escape even if only to return to his cellar room. There he immediately pulled off his jacket, which he wasn't certain now he would ever want to wear again. He now, for some reason, didn't even want to keep his gold medal in the pocket. He would just store it in the drawer in the chest where he had hidden the money from Mr. Fitzbottom to be used if he ran away. He reached into the pocket to pull the medal out, only to find the pocket empty. His precious gold medal was gone!

 # Chapter XIII

In which Max's running-away roller coaster has hit rock
bottom. It can go no lower, and he must make his decision
to do something about it at last, but deciding and doing
are two very different things.

This was it! This was the last straw! Max's
running-away roller coaster had been going up
and down so many times he had lost count. But
now, on top of all else, that big bully Snitch, who
was apparently going to be "learnin'" him how to clean
"terlits" and everything else forever just to get out of the
work himself, was also proved to a thief. For who else
could have taken the gold medal? He could easily have
taken it when he'd made trips down to the cellar minus
Max to use Max's washroom, and simply come into his
unlocked room and helped himself to the medal. But try
and prove it! No, Max knew he'd never see his medal
again.

Well, he had been ordered around by that big
monster moron Snitch for long enough, and it began to
look as if it could go on forever. From what he overheard,
it didn't seem as if Delilah was ever going to return. And
if Snitch could do the work for probably the lowest pay

imaginable, and had someone working for him for no pay at all, why should the pinchpenny Measley's change this splendid arrangement?

And then on top of all that, he had to put on his Ballyhoo jacket and perform like a trained circus monkey for those two horrors, the Measley girls. Chocolates they wanted to give him for spying! He had said "yes" because he knew he could make up some crazy tales to tell them. So why not say "yes"? What difference did it make?

Well, now Max made his decision. He would run away that very night! It had to be night because in the daylight he'd risk being caught by the two goons, Digger and Dork, who patrolled Measley Manor. Max only wished he could let Moose know. Moose had had him over for pizza several evenings, and Max had come to pretty much like him. And, of course, he was crazy about Moxie and Mojo, and he knew they were almost as crazy about him as they were Moose. He wanted to explain to them why he had to do what he was about to do. But maybe he'd write Moose a letter, and he could try to explain it all to the dogs.

Max knew he'd have to travel light, so decided he could only take one of his two suitcases. He intended to wait until the dead of night, of course, but would have his suitcase packed and ready. So trying not to think of what might lie ahead. He started to pack.

Even though his Ballyhoo jacket now had unpleasant memories, he knew he might want it later, so it was the first thing he packed at the bottom of the suitcase. Then came clean underwear, another sweatshirt, and his second pair of jeans which he had never worn. He was actually wearing the same pair he'd worn all along as no one had offered to throw them in any laundry. But he suddenly decided to take them off and wear the new pair. Which is why he somehow saw something he'd managed to miss seeing before, a tiny corner of a piece of folded white paper in his back pocket. Max pulled it out, unfolded it and saw that it was a note, and that it was from Mrs. Dumpty. It was the note he'd forgotten all about! He sat down on his cot to read it.

"Dear Max, some afternoon when Snitch has left for the day, please do come and see me. I would very much like to talk to you. Just knock when you come. Sincerely, your friend, Mrs. Dumpty."

What could Mrs. Dumpty have wanted to say to him? He'd been back to clean, sweep and dust several times with Snitch. Mrs. Dumpty had given him searching looks each time, but never said anything to him about the note. Well, how could she with Snitch hovering over him every minute?

Now Max would never knew what she'd wanted, and what was almost worse, his Ballyhoo manners should have had him either appear, or write a note back. But it was too late now. He would be gone, and that was that.

But he put the note in his suitcase anyway.

Once his suitcase was packed, the money from Mr. Fitzbottom in his pocket, he turned down the tiny dim lamp by his cot, and lay down to wait until he could feel certain he would be the only one up and around at Measley Manor. He wished there was a full moon out, but half a moon was better than no moon. Once it was high enough up in the sky is when he would leave.

Finally, he decided it was time. He turned off the little lamp, crept across the floor, picked up his suitcase, and opened the door, intending to make his way down the dark hallway. But he had only opened his door a crack, when he swiftly and silently closed it again, his heart thumping. Then he opened it again the tiniest crack and looked down the hallway.

The door with the big padlock was wide open and there was a light on in the room. It came from a bare bulb dangling from the ceiling. Max could see a big trunk with two paper sacks and two bottles sitting on top of it.

As he was watching, in stumped Digger and Dork from outside, both carrying big shovels and lanterns.

They stood the shovels up against the back wall, set the lanterns on the floor, picked up paper sacks and bottles, and sat themselves down on the trunk. Moments later, they were eating what looked like enormous submarine sandwiches from the sacks, and drinking from the bottles.

Max continued to watch as they sat there eating, drinking and talking. They were not trying to keep their loud voices down, but as they were mostly talking with their mouths full, Max couldn't tell what they were saying. But it didn't seem as if they'd been out doing gardening at that time of night. So why the shovels? Max concluded that this was weird with a capital "W". But beyond weird, this put a big foot down on his plans.

Frightened lest they might decide to come down the cellar passageway, perhaps to use the washroom, Max quietly shut his door. Then, in the dark, by only the dim light of the moon coming in his window, he began putting his clothes back, even hanging his Ballyhoo jacket on the same nails. If Snitch came charging rudely into the room as he often did, he had better see things just as they'd always been.

But then things got even weirder. He had undressed, and was ready to climb into his bed, when he happened to look out the window. Walking right by, both carrying flashlights, were no other than the Measley twins, Ruby and Pearl! They were wearing long black coats, and with their faces almost hidden by black, broad=brimmed hats. They disappeared into the building. Minutes later, they reappeared with Digger and Dork, carrying their shovels and lanterns.

Why this hour of the night? And why shovels? And it was then Max remembered the old cemetery Moose told him about. Max actually had been a little spooked by the idea of going there, but if Mojo and Moxie had fun there playing around the old gravestones, then that's where he intended to go. Was it possible that's where Digger and Dork had been, and now were headed back with the

94

Measley girls? What could they be planning, or maybe just hoping to dig up? Or...bury?

Would he be around to ever find out? On the other hand, what did it matter anyway? What did matter was that running away at night might be hazardous to his health if the goons and the Measley's were out prowling.

The question now was, could he ever run away safely *ever?*

 Chapter XIV

In which Max makes use of his invitation to visit Mrs.
Dumpty, and is glad that his jeans never made it to the
laundry

L ate that very next afternoon, Max knocked at
Mrs. Dumpty's door.

"Come on in!" Mrs. Dumpty's voice sang
out.

Max cautiously opened the door and peered in.
Mrs. Dumpty in another bright pink shirt, slacks, and
stocking feet was seated in a chair by the window again.
She beckoned to Max.

"Come on!" she said. "Come right on in, darlin'! I
was wondering why I'd never had any reply to my note.
I've really wanted to talk to you, young man."

Max decided he should be completely honest. "I...I
put the note in my jeans pocket, and so much other stuff
has happened, I guess I just forgot about it."

"Well," said Mrs. Dumpty indignantly, "I can just
imagine the 'stuff' you've been going through. I don't
approve the way Snitch torments you, darlin'. But I must
tell you the truth, though, I do feel sorry for him as well.
I don't think he has a very happy home life from what

Delilah has said. But it's *you* I wanted to talk about, Max. You clearly don't belong here. I and all the others are quite aware of that. We may be old, but we're not blind. Now tell me, how old are you, Max."

"Eleven," replied Max.

"And so we all thought," said Mrs. Dumpty. "And is Max short for Maximilian?"

Max nodded.

"Is that your full name, darlin'?" asked Mrs. Dumpty.

Max shook his head. "No, it's actually Maximilian Pettigrew Westmorington Bassford Thorndike Finstersill Smith the Fifth," he said, and expected Mrs. Dumpty to burst out laughing and say something like "You've got to be kidding!"

Instead she said, "Why am I not surprised? Anyway, I'm pretty curious about things. Always have been. Can't tell you why except perhaps it's because I once wrote stories. All I know is you don't look like a young man who should be doing what you're doing, so I'm wondering why you are. Having to be taught how to lift a toilet seat...merciful heavens! Where did the Measley ladies, if you can call them that, find you anyway?"

"I...I...I'm Moose's cousin," replied Max. "Sort of."

"Moose our handyman?" asked Mrs. Dumpty.

Max nodded.

"What does 'sort of' mean?" asked Mrs. Dumpty. "I've never heard of a 'sort of' cousin, or any other kind of 'sort of' relative."

"Well, Mr. Fitzbottom told me he was a fifth cousin twice removed," said Max. "I don't know what that is exactly. It's in some Bible Moose has, but I'm not sure it's his Bible, or that he's my cousin, or why he even agreed o take me."

"I don't know Moose very well, darlin'," said Mrs. Dumpty, "but from what I do know, he seems like a very lovely intelligent man. I've often wondered what he's doing here as well. Don't know why, I only have a feeling that Bible really is his, and you really are a fifth cousin twice removed. But why was this Mr. Fitzbottom needing to find someone to take you? Where are you parents, darlin'?"

Max shuffled his feet on the carpet. If he told Mrs. Dumpty the truth, wouldn't she just say the same thing as that awful Mitzi Fiddle, that he was the biggest liar who ever lived? Who in the world ever had a father who put his whole enormous fortune into a resort on an island in the Pacific Ocean, and then lost it in a humongous earthquake that went down and took him and his only son's mother right down with it to the bottom of the ocean?

Max decided to put one toe into the story by way of a feeler. "They're at the bottom of ocean," he said.

"Now that's quite a remarkable place to be," said Mrs. Dumpty. "Would you mind telling me how they got there?"

And so right then and there to the wrinkled old person exactly like the kind that had always given him the creeps, Max poured out the whole story of Rainbow's End, and everything else about his life, including The Golden Truffle, Ballyhoo, and even Pencival and his father's toilet and tub company, which Max was so horror stricken to find in Mrs. Dumpty's and all the other old people's very own bathrooms.

Max told her every last bit, and when he finished, he hung his head and waited for Mrs. Dumpty to let him know what a big liar he was. But all he heard was the sound of sniffling. He looked up and saw tears streaming down her face.

"That's the saddest story I've ever heard," she said, dabbing her eyes with a tiny lace handkerchief.

"Do you mean you really believe me?" gasped Max.

"Of course, I believe you, darlin'!" said Mrs. Dumpty. "Who could ever make up a far-out story like that one? I'm a writer and I could never have done it. And you're only eleven, for goodness sake! You're not a young genius book writer by any chance, are you?"

Max shook his head.

"I didn't really think so," said Mrs. Dumpty. "But if your story is true, and I absolutely believe it is, well, I have to say I think it's a disgraceful thing that Mr. Fitzbottom could not have done a better job of finding you a home. Well, of course, as I said, I believe that Moose is a fine man and shouldn't be doing what he's doing either. I confess I don't understand any of this. But, oh, you poor, poor thing. My heart goes out to you, darlin'. It does indeed!"

With those words from Mrs. Dumpty, the most terrible thing happened. Max, despite all that had happened to him, had somehow never shed a single tear. Not one! But now this wrinkled old person with the loony name of Mrs. Dumpty had pulled the plug. For some reason, he felt that this was the first person who knew way deep down, deep as the ocean where he had lost his parents, how he felt. And calling him a poor, poor thing! Nobody had ever said that to him. Not a single person! Not once!

Perhaps it was because he was so rotten spoiled no one bothered to say it. Perhaps it was because he had never shown that he *needed* to hear it. But he did! He *did*! So now Max stood in front of Mrs. Dumpty with tears running down his cheeks just as tears had run down hers.

"Oh, you poor darlin'," said Mrs. Dumpty. "I didn't mean to make you cry. But you know I just suspected something about you, and I was right. The others here all agree with me, too. If only I could do something about it, but I can't. Just come see me any time as you would your grandmother."

"I...I've never had a grandmother," said Max, wiping his eyes on his sweatshirt sleeve. "My grandparents were all gone before I was old enough to know them."

"Well, you have one now!" exclaimed Mrs. Dumpty. "And I hope you'll drop in to see me often, won't you?"

Max nodded, and then, almost before he knew what he was doing, suddenly said, "May I help you put on your shoes, Mrs. Dumpty?"

"Why that would be lovely, darlin'!" exclaimed Mrs. Dumpty.

Max could hardly believe he had done this, once again helping a wrinkled old person put on her shoes. But he had offered, and he did it, and somehow, it didn't feel creepy at all. But he was confused about his feelings as ever as he dashed a remaining tear from his cheek and left the room.

And found Mitzi Fiddle leaning on the opposite wall, arms folded, staring right at him!

Chapter XV

In which Max continues to learn that things are seldom what they seem, even if it's not just skim milk masquerading as cream, and maybe even someone named Mitzi.

"What...what are *you* doing here?" Max said with his jaw clenched.

"I just happened to be coming down the hall," replied Mitzi. "No law against that far as I know. I also just happened to see you going into Mrs. Dumpty's room. I know Snitch has left for the day, so I just wondered what you were doing and why, and I decided to wait and find out."

"So I suppose you're going to run right with this piece of information to the Measley's!" Max hurled at her.

"What in heck are you talking about?' asked Mitzi. "Have you gone over the edge or something?"

"Oh, I know all about it," said Max. "They told me how you agreed to spy for them for...for chocolates!"

"Holy cow! What kind of lamebrain do you think I am?" said Mitzi. "Spying for chocolates! But might I ask why they told you that?"

"Why do you think?" said Max. "They were trying to get me to do it as well."

"And what did you say?" Mitzi asked.

"Same as you, that I'd do it," said Max.

"And were you going to do it?" said Mitzi.

"What do *you* think?" said Max. "I just figured I had to say yes, or they'd end up having someone spying on me, just like you're doing."

"Well, to begin with," said Mitzi, "I'm no moron and I figured exactly the same thing. But what made them think I was such an idiot I'd spy for

chocolates? Are they nuts, or something? Is that what they offered you?"

"Of course," said Max. "But I told them I'd like money instead."

"And they agreed to that?" said Mitzi.

"Oh, yeah, sure they did," said Max. "I told them chocolate makes me break out in spots."

"Does it?" asked Mitzi.

"No," said Max.

"Golly," said Mitzi, "why didn't I think of that? Of course, it doesn't matter anyway as neither of us is going to do it. I'm sure not!"

"But I'm going to make up some stories, anyway," said Max.

"Wow!" said Mitzi. "You're sharp. I never thought of that."

"Well, I want to earn the money. I might need it," said Max.

"To use when you run away, I suppose," said Mitzi. "Are you still planning to try that idiotic idea?"

Max just shrugged and decided he wouldn't tell her how he already had tried. And not even about what he'd seen the two goons doing. Not yet, anyway. After all, until about five minutes ago, they'd been at each other's throats.

"So okay," he said, "now tell me why were you waiting around to see me anyway?"

"I will," replied Mitzi. "But first tell me why you were crying when you came out of Mrs. Dumpty's room. What did she say to you?"

"Who said I was crying?" said Max.

"You're eyes are red, and you were wiping something off your face," said Mitzi. "That looks like crying to me."

"That's all you know," said Max. "Are you from outer space or something? Haven't you ever heard of someone getting dust in their eyes?"

"If you say so," replied Mitzi.

"Anyway," said Max, "so now answer my question. What did you want to see me about?"

"Oh, I just found out something," she said, and got suddenly very interested in picking at a fingernail.

"That I'm really an escaped criminal or something?" said Max.

"No," said Mitzi. "It's just that I found out that crazy story you told me the day we met might be true."

"H...how did you find that out?" stammered Max.

"Well, Moose was in the kitchen yesterday and he and Mum got to talking while I was there. He told Mum the story he'd told the Measley witches he had to make up so they'd let you come here. He told her the real story, which happened to be the same one you told."

"So now you don't think I'm the biggest liar who ever lived?" said Max.

Mitzi grinned. "Well, I don't know about that. I'll have to see, but at the moment, I guess I'd have to say you're probably not. That's a pretty crazy story, though, you have to admit."

Max finally grinned back. "Yes, I guess it is."

"Anyway," Mitzi said, "if you really had a chauffeur to drive you to that Ballybooboo school..."

Max gave a deep sigh. "That's Ballyhoo," he said.

"Okay, Ballyhoo," said Mitzi. But if you really had a chauffeur and a butler and all that stuff, this must be pretty awful for you. I mean, living in that cell in the basement, and working for Snitch. He tells Mum he's 'learnin' you to clean, especially 'terlits'."

Max was forced to grin. "Yeah," he said, "he even starts with telling me the first thing I 'got to do' is lift the lid, and he says it in a loud voice so everyone can find out how clever he is. The old people must think I'm some kind of half-wit."

"I expect they know better," said Mitzi. "They're pretty smart. Anyway, I feel kind of sorry for Snitch sometimes. He came in once with one side of his face all black and blue, and one eye swollen shut. Delilah told Mum he has a sick mother with three small kids to look after, and that Snitch's pa beats him regularly. Snitch has had to go to work, and hasn't even finished high school."

"Sounds like some made-up soap opera story," said Max. "Do you believe all that?"

"You would if you'd seen him," said Mitzi.

Max just shrugged. Too bad for Snitch, but that didn't make working under him any better. And how about stealing? Max wasn't ready to talk about that yet, though.

"Anyway," Mitzi said, and started staring down at a toe making circles in the carpet, "I wouldn't blame you for thinking about running way, but I hope you don't."

"Why would you care if I did or I didn't?" Max said,

Mitzi continued making carpet circles. "Oh, I don't know. I just think it's neat having you here. Maybe we can do stuff together later. And...and if you must know, I like that Ballybooboo...I mean, Ballyhoo jacket you were wearing. It's really cool."

"I'm not so sure I like it anymore," said Max. "Not after the Measley's made me wear it yesterday to show me off to somebody who might be coming to live here."

Mitzi's jaw fell. "They really did that?"

"Oh sure," said Max.

"Well, I hope you'll wear it again anyway. I really do think it's cool."

106

"I can't exactly wear it for my job cleaning 'terlits' for Snitch," said Max. "But I'll wear it sometime, if you like," he added carelessly. That jacket suddenly began looking pretty good to him all of a sudden. Cool, actually.

"Look," said Mitzi, "would you like to do something together some time after you get off work?"

"Are you asking me for a date?" asked Max.

"Don't be an idiot," said Mitzi.

"Well, what then?" said Max.

"I just thought you'd like to go exploring," said Mitzi,

"Exploring where?" asked Max.

Mitzi shrugged. "Oh just someplace around. You're not afraid of spooky places, are you?"

"Not that I know of, " said Max. "Why? Do you have someplace in mind?"

"Maybe," said Mitzi. "So do you want to or not?"

"Sure, why not?" said Max. "I mean, if I'm still around."

"You're not planning to run away or do something dumb like that without letting me know, are you?" said Mitzi.

"Look," said Max, "when and if I decide to run away, you'll be the first to know. You can throw me a going-away party. Okay?"

"So how about Saturday? No school and I'll be here helping Mum," Mitzi said.

"I'll have to check my calendar," said cool-guy Max. Then he grinned.

Mitzi returned the grin. "So come pick me up in the kitchen around three. Okay?'

"Sure, why not?" said more cool-guy Max.

"Well, I've got to go now. Mum's waiting for me." Mitzi started to run down the hall, then stopped and looked back. "For your information, I should let you know I don't like secrets!"

"If I have any to reveal, I will," said Max. "Ballyhoo honor!"

"Okay then," said Mitzi with another grin, "I guess that's as good as anything, Ballyhoo boy!"

Well, how about *that*! Maybe, thought Max, it was a good thing he hadn't tried to wash out his jeans and never found Mrs. Dumpty's note. Yes, indeed, just how *about* that!

 # Chapter XVI

In which another event happens that deepens the mystery but still doesn't explain why Digger and Dork were prowling about with shovels and lanterns, not to mention the Measley girls arriving looking like ghouls.

M ax's running-away roller coaster was now definitely stalled. Of course, he had to admit to himself that it wasn't entirely because he might run right into Digger and Dork or the Measley girls in escaping Measley Manor at night. His decision to hang around a while longer just might, he had to admit to himself, have something to do with Mrs. Dumpty and that it seemed he might actually have a friend. Mitzi was a girl, that was true, but a friend is a friend, and all Max had ever had in that category was Pencival. If you could call him that!

What Max wondered was why he hadn't told Mitzi about the Measley girls, dressed like ghouls, and the goons wandering about at night with shovels and lanterns. Could it be because he didn't want her to know about the attempt he'd already made at running away? Well, he could have just said he was looking out his window without saying how what he saw had made his plans go up in smoke. No, he'd probably have to tell her the truth. Ballyhoo honor!

How about that invitation to go exploring. That could be a good time to spring it on her. And on further thought, could asking him if he was afraid of spooky places have anything to do with the cemetery? The plot was definitely thickening.

Then that night something happened that added to his list another something weird he would report to Mitzi. Things were definitely getting weirder and weirder around this place. The plot could be thickening even further.

Max was in his room that night lying in bed, still dressed but with his sneakers off, reading the ratty copy of Dicken's *Bleak House* he'd borrowed from Moose, when he heard scuffling noises outside his door. It *had* to be the goons again, he thought. He turned off his light and posted himself at the window to see if they would leave with their shovels, or if the Measley girls showed up again.

Instead, he saw what looked like a bunch of people leaving the building.

Actually, it looked like...no it couldn't be. But there was no doubt in his mind that it was!

What would *they* be doing out this time of night? He kept on looking, hypnotized, as the group went creeping toward the forest, which was toward the cemetery, of course. A few yards away from the building, and flashlights were turned on. It looked like a lot of fireflies bobbing up and down moving farther and farther away.

What kind of craziness were they up to? Didn't they know the Measley girls and the goons might be showing up any time? Well, no, why *would* they? Not unless Max had told them, which he hadn't. But he knew now that he *had* to warn them. And ASAP! There was no time to lose. Shoving his feet back into his sneakers, and tying them with trembling fingers, he first checked to make sure no one was in the hall, then he flew down and out the door.

He didn't know how he would approach them without scaring them half to death, but there was no way to do it but just *do* it.

"Hey, you Mother Goose-ites, what do you think you're doing?"

They all stopped at once, their faces frozen.

Mrs. Dumpty unfroze first. "We're on a mission, darlin'" she said. Her voice was a bit shaky, which made Max feel terrible.

"You're not going to report us, son, are you?" asked Officer Dickory. He sounded rather shaky as well. "We...we weren't doing anything...er...illegal."

"Max wouldn't do anything like that, would you, darlin'?" asked Mrs. Dumpty.

"We were just...just out for a night stroll," said Dr. Humpty in a fading voice.

"That's right...a little stroll," the others all chimed in eagerly. They seemed to have forgotten what Mrs. Dumpty said about a "mission".

"Look," said Max trying to sound stern, but was feeling pretty shaky himself. "I don't have to know what you're really doing. It's none of my business and I don't care." Max was lying, naturally. He actually cared a great deal.

"I only came out to warn you," he said. "I haven't told anyone, but last night I saw Digger and Dork leaving the building with shovels and lanterns. And then the Measley's arrived all dressed in black, I suppose so they'd less likely be spotted by anyone. I don't know what they were doing or where they were going, but what I believe is they might be back tonight doing again what they were doing last night, and I don't think they were just out for a...a *stroll!*"

The group all looked at one another.

"Could they be doing the same thing we're doing?" asked Ms. Bo Peep.

"But why would they be when they don't have the..." Dr. Doodle stopped in mid-sentence.

"Maybe there's more than one," said Mrs. Diddle.

"I think we should tell Max what this is all about," said Mrs. Dumpty.

"No offense," said Commander King Cole, "but he *is* just a boy, and the Measley's can be powerfully persuasive..."

"Yes, just a boy who risked coming out to warn us, and in whom I believe the Measley's have met their match, Commander," said Mrs. Dumpty. "Max, please come to my room at four p.m. tomorrow, won't you, darlin', and we'll explain what this is all about."

"Are you sure about this, Mrs. Dumpty?" asked Dr. Mrs. Muffet.

"Never been surer about anything in my life!" replied Mrs. Dumpty. "So will you be there, darlin'?"

Max hesitated, and then finally nodded. "But...but right now," he said, "I think you had all better return to the building. It's too risky staying out here. I guess you *do* have keys to get back in?"

They all looked at one another. Apparently they'd forgotten about having to get back in the building!

"You see, Commander," said Mrs. Dumpty as they all trailed Max back to the Manor. "Now you just tell me again, if you dare, about Max being 'just a boy'!"

 # Chapter XVII

In which Max goes to the meeting in Mrs. Dumpty's room, and gets more than just explanations about the night prowlers.

Max arrived breathlessly at Mrs. Dumpty's door at several minutes after four. He had run all the way from his room, scared that he might bump into the Measley's prowling the halls. Mrs. Dumpty peered out cautiously before opening the door a crack just wide enough for him to slip through. And Max found himself the object of the nine pairs of eyes belonging to nine people who had somehow managed to pack themselves into Mrs. Dumpty's room.

Max was now familiar with all of them, or, if truth be known, was more familiar with their "terlits", of which he had thorough knowledge thanks to the expert teaching of Snitch. But now, of course, he felt part of their conspiracy, if conspiracy it was, although he had yet to find out what it was all about. The plot had indeed thickened!

The nine people in Mrs. Dumpty's room were:

Commander King Cole, the naval officer

Ms. Bo Peep, detective

Coach Winkie, basketball coach
Dr. Mrs. Muffet, anthropologist
Dr. Humpty, professor of astronomy
Mrs. Diddle, prize-winning artist
Officer Dickory, medal-winning police officer
Dr. Doodle, veterinarian
Mr. Tweedle-dee, animal trainer

"Max," said Mrs. Dumpty, "I believe you've met all these nice people, who are very grateful to you for taking the big risk to yourself of warning us last night. And I want to tell you that they all agree with me completely that you shouldn't be here doing what you're doing, especially as I've told them your sad story. I hope you don't mind that I've done that, do you, darlin'?"

Max could only shake his head for he hardly knew what to say.

"But have you ever asked him that other question?" asked Ms. Bo Peep.

"Oh dear, I'm afraid not," said Mrs. Dumpty.

"Well, hadn't you better?" said Mrs. Diddle. "There is one thing, they all rather wanted to know, darlin', and I suppose I should have asked you," said Mrs. Dumpty. "To be truthful, have the Measley girls talked to you about...well, doing any special favors for them and then, well, rewarding you for doing them? They've made such offers to others of us here, and naturally they've been turned down. But we all think it...well, that it might be very difficult for someone your age suddenly finding yourself in this terrible life to refuse. And now especially after what you found us doing last night, and remembering what Commander King Cole mentioned about how persuasive the Measley girls can be..."

"If...if...if what you're talking about is tattling, well, they *have* asked me. And I told them 'yes" I'd do it!" said Max.

There were ten collective gasps of horror from everyone.

It was all Max could do to keep a straight face.

114

"But Officer Dickory," Max said, "I'd like to ask you something. I guess you know a lot about criminals. Do you know of any criminal who might be going to rob a house, or even a bank, and comes to tell you which house or which bank he plans to rob, and when he plans to do it?"

"That would be pretty stupid," said Officer Dickory.

"So," said Max, "why would I tell you I'm going to be spying for the Measley's if I'm really going to? If you all want to know, the reason I said 'yes' is that I suddenly had this great idea right while they were asking me. I'm going to make up stories to tell them. I've even thought of a couple. I could tell them Dr. Humpty is secretly planning to go on the next trip to the moon, or Commander King Cole is planning to sail around the world in a sailboat all by himself. You can all help me make up stories. Serve them right!"

The collective looks of horror on ten faces were suddenly transformed into ten collective looks of surprise, followed by wide smiles.

"There, you see!" said Mrs. Dumpty triumphantly. "Only a boy, indeed! I just knew I wasn't making a mistake."

"Of course, you weren't!" said Coach Winkie. "We really knew it all along."

"Yes, we did!"

"Certainly, we did!"

"Not know it all along? Why the very idea!"

Nobody wanted to be left out of letting everyone else know that they never had had any doubt about it, and how clever Max was to have come up with the idea, and why hadn't anyone else thought of it. It was quite a while before everyone settled back down.

"I suppose they offered you chocolates?" said Ms. Bo Peep.

"Oh yes," said Max. "I told them chocolates make me break out in spots. I asked for money instead."

"And those skinflints actually agreed to that?" said Mrs. Diddle.

"They said 'yes'," said Max.

"What a clever boy!" said Dr. Humpty. "And what do you propose to do with the money?"

Max looked down at the toes of his shoes for help, but didn't get much from that source. "I...I thought I might need it when I...I run away."

"Run away!" several voices cried at once.

"Oh, but you can't do that, darlin'," said Mrs. Dumpty. "We want you to stay, we do indeed!"

Everyone nodded hard, and nodded, and nodded yet again.

"Yes!"

"Yes!"

"Yes!"

"You mustn't even think about it!"

"We won't let you go, will we?"

"No!"

"No!"

"No!"

"Oh well," said Max. "It's not definite. As I said, I'm only just *thinking* about it."

"Well, please do stop thinking about it, darlin'" said Mrs. Dumpty. "We don't want to hear another word about it. You're the one bright spot that's come into our lives in a long time. You know, don't you that unless Moose takes us on the bus on an emergency trip to town, we're never allowed out of the building. Didn't I tell you that?"

Max shook his head.

"Well, it's true," said Coach Winkie. "Why do you suppose I have a basketball hanging from a door in my room?"

"Or why I only paint pictures mostly of the scene from my window?" said Mrs. Diddle.

"Or why I can only look through my telescope from my room?" said Dr. Humpty.

"It's been this way since the Measley girls took over Dolly Manor from the Dolly's and turned it into Measley Manor," said Dr. Mrs. Muffet.

"Yes, and now gone and hired those two horrors, Digger and Dork, to patrol the grounds," said Mrs. Diddle. "It's supposed to be to keep out intruders, but we all know it's to keep us in. We've all suspected there's just something they don't want us to find or find out."

"And what you've told us about their night excursion pretty much confirms that, wouldn't you all say?'"

All nodded at once.

"But we'll talk about that shortly," said Mrs. Dumpty. "I know Max must want to learn why *we* were out there having a…a stroll. First I think it would be fun to let him know about the little something we do for entertainment and to keep out spirits up as well. Don't you think we should?"

All heads in the room nodded.

"Well, Max, darlin'," said Mrs. Dumpty. "The something we do is fortune telling. And I'm the one that does it, so you can help me carry out my crystal ball from my closet."

"It's not really a crystal ball," she whispered to him as she brought down from the closet shelf a cut crystal bowl filled with scraps of paper. "These are just fortunes from fortune cookies I saved over the years. I believe most passionately in fortune cookie fortunes."

"Me too," said Max. "Does everyone know that's where the fortunes come from?"

"Oh, I suspect they do, as I may have dropped a hint or two," said Mrs. Dumpty. "But nobody wants to spoil the fun by mentioning it. At any rate, what I say is that a fortune is a fortune is a fortune, even if it comes from a cookie. Don't you agree?"

"I do," said Max, who actually did.

When they emerged from the closet, Mrs. Dumpty returned to her chair and Max dropped down on the floor beside her.

"Now, darlin'," she said. "You hold the bowl for me while I say the magic words over it so it will give up the fortunes."

"Abracadabra," she said, closing her eyes and waving her hand over the bowl. "Tell us our fortunes, oh wonderful bowl!"

Then she dipped her hand into the bowl, and pulled out a scrap of paper.

Closing her eyes and waving her other hand over the paper, she said, "This fortune is for Commander King Cole."

Then she opened her eyes and read, "The skills you have learned will one day come in handy."

"Splendid!" said Commander King Cole. "Just the thing to know for that trip I plan to go sailing solo around the world!"

This brought laughs all around.

Mrs. Dumpty continued pulling fortune-cookie fortunes from her bowl, and something was said about ever one.

For Ms. Bo Peep: "You will have a very remarkable and rewarding surprise."

Was it to find an exciting fingerprint, perhaps?

For Coach Winkie: "Your skill will soon bring skills to another."

Could the "another" be Max shooting baskets?

For Dr. Mrs. Muffet: "A thrilling time is in your immediate future."

Would somebody bring her an exciting artifact some day?

For Dr. Humpty: "You will find something amazing if you keep looking."

Could he be the one to discover a new star in his window telescope?

For Mrs. Diddle: "Your past success will be overshadowed by your future success."

Could she enter one of the paintings of the view from her window in a contest and win a prize?

For Officer Dickory: "Do not be surprised if you have an exciting event in your future."

Would he hunt down a wanted criminal, and earn another medal?

For Dr. Doodle: "Your skills might once again be useful."

Would she be able to take care of Moxie and Mojo some day?

For Mr. Tweedle-dee: "Something you love will return to your life."

Would he be allowed to train Moxie and Mojo so they wouldn't lose all their good manners?

For Mrs. Dumpty herself: "Your skill will accomplish what many other cannot."

Could it be that Mrs. Dumpty might make all their fortunes come true?

Max sitting there holding the bowl was beginning to have some very mixed-up feelings about his former old-people thoughts. It seemed to him that they were all stuck here, not even allowed to walk outside, and yet they all managed to be pleased with their ridiculous "fortunes" which hadn't the chance of a snowflake in summer of coming true.

"And now, darlin', here's one for you," said Mrs. Dumpty, breaking into his thoughts.

"There is yet time for you to take a different path," she read.

So there it was, thought Max. If this didn't make up his mind about making another attempt at running away, what would?

But the same thought must have occurred to all of the rest of them in the room.

"I don't like that fortune at all," said Dr. Doodle.

"Well, I certainly don't," said Commander King Cole.

"I think he should have a second one," said Ms. Bo Peep. "All in favor raise their right hand."

Every right hand in the room was raised. Hesitantly, Max raised his as well. Back into the bowl went Mrs. Dumpty's hand.

"Abracadabra!" said Mrs. Dumpty with closed eyes. The room fell silent, no one saying a word as she rummaged and rummaged in the bowl, and finally pulled out a fortune.

"Depart not from the place to which fate has brought you, and you will have thrilling events unfold in your life."

Smiles replaced the worried looks on every face in the room.

"Well then, that's settled!" said Commander King Cole cheerfully.

Max could hardly help grinning himself, even though in his mind the subject had not exactly been settled.

"Now that we've done fortunes," said Ms. Bo Peep, "aren't we going to explain to Max why we were out...um...strolling in the forest at night?"

"Well, we've all agreed that we should," said Commander King Cole, "including me. So I believe he needs to see the map."

"What...what map is that?" Max asked.

"A document I found hidden way in the back of my closet, darlin'" said Mrs. Dumpty. "It simply fell on the floor one day when I was pulling something off a shelf. We all decided it could be a map of everything around Measley Manor."

"There are some markings on it which we believe might lead to something interesting around here," said Officer Dickory. "We think it's why the Measley girls don't want us prowling around."

120

"Yes, and hired those two goons to see that we don't!" exclaimed Dr. Doodle.

Max sat frozen as his conversation with the Measley girls slowly played back in his head. "Just let us know if anything unusual is going on that we should know about if anyone finds some...er...curious old papers like maps that really belong to us."

"What is it, Max, darlin'?" asked Mrs. Dumpty.

Max had to swallow and swallow again before he could squeeze out the words. "When the Measley's tried to get me to promise about spying, they told me to let them know if...if anyone finds some...some...curious old papers like maps that really belong to them."

This revelation was greeted with a stunned silence.

"Well, Officer Dickory, does it?" asked Ms. Bo Peep.

Officer Dickory thought this over. "I'd have to say it probably belongs to whoever occupied this room once. We'll...ahem...make an effort to find the owner, of course."

"But that won't be easy, will it?" asked Mr. Tweedle-dee. "We're not allowed to go anywhere."

"Exactly," said Officer Dickory. "So we'll just hang on to it until we find the rightful owner. If the Measley's don't let us go anywhere to do this, so be it. And may I suggest we all just keep our mouths tightly shut on the matter? Are we all agreed on this? Might I have a show of hands?"

All hands were raised, including the hand of Max, even though he was not officially a member of the Mother Goose-ites.

"But the question remains," said Coach Winkie. "How are we going to do anything about the telltale markings if we can't leave the building to go exploring? We all think it might have something to do with the old cemetery, but what is anyone's guess?"

Max hesitated and then cleared his throat. And then cleared it again.

"Yes, darlin'?" said Mrs. Dumpty. "Would you like to say something about this?"

"Well, would you trust me with the map? Well, me and Mitzi, that is. She's invited me to go exploring."

Glances were exchanged around the room.

"Exploring where, Max darlin'?" asked Mrs. Dumpty.

"I have no idea," replied Max. "She did ask if I was afraid of spooky places. That sounds like a cemetery to me."

"We do trust you, Max," said Officer Dickory, "but I'm afraid we don't know about Mitzi. She's a nice young person, but how do we know the Measley's haven't gotten to her with their spying proposals."

"Oh, they have!" said Max. Then he grinned soon as he saw the looks of dismay on all the Goose-ite faces. "But she gave them a bunch of hooey just the way I did. Said she'd do it for chocolates, but she thinks it's a big joke. If you trust me, I know you can trust her as well."

"Then I say we let the two of them have the map," said Commander King Cole. "Can we have another show of hands?"

All hands went up. And so it was settled. Mrs. Dumpty went to her closet, and returned with a folded piece of paper, stained and brown with age. It crackled as she unfolded it and handed it to Max. The old people were right. It did look as if it could be a map of Measley Manor or at least a building that might have once stood in the same place, and the land surrounding it, going all the way down to the shore. A faded X in the middle of it could be about the location of the old cemetery.

"You'll take good care of it, won't you, darlin'?" said Mrs. Dumpty.

Those really cool, nice old people trusting him with their precious map? You bet Max would take good care of it! He would guard it with his life.

It would stay right on his personal person in his jeans pocket. Snitch, the Measley girls and the goons would have to kill him to get to it.

As for the running-away roller coaster. Well, for the moment it had definitely inched way back up from rock bottom. After all, what if that second fortune proved to be right?

Chapter XVIII

In which Max explains "all" to Mitzi, they go exploring
with Moxie and Mojo, and find a definite connection
between a cemetery and some very suspicious and
sinister shovel activity.

It was a good thing Saturday was only the next day after Max met with the Mother Goose-ites, and left the room with the precious, and it must be said, *super mysterious* map in his jeans pocket. He had actually folded the jeans and slept with them under his pillow. He was going to take no chances of having it away from his person for more than the time it took to climb into his pajamas. No way! No how!

He was busting at the seams to talk to Mitzi. Wait until she heard all that he had to tell her! And all the while he was counting the hours until he saw her, he was putting two and two together. Digger and Dork with shovels and lanterns. The Measley girls crawling around at night. Mitzi asking him if he was afraid of spooky places. The old map with what looked liked markings that might mean something very important. It all added up to CEMETERY!

Did shovels mean digging up...what...bodies? Max decided he wouldn't think about that. Not yet anyway. Well, it didn't involve *his* body, did it? Better not think about that interesting idea either.

As soon as Max poked his head into the kitchen, caught Mitzi's eye and motioned her out, they crept out and down the stairs to his room, which Max decided was the safest place to "reveal all".

"Wow!" said Mitzi. "Is this where you actually live?"

"Yeah," said Max. "The Taj Mahal!"

"It might not be forever," said Mitzi hopefully, then less hopefully, "Will it?"

"I'm not planning on it," said Max.

"You're not still thinking of that loony idea of running away, are you?" said Mitzi.

"Does it matter?" asked Max.

"I thought I had made that clear, stupid," replied Mitzi.

Max shrugged. "Well, I...I don't know. The subject is...still on the table. But what I was referring to was Mrs. Dumpty's fortune cookie fortune for me."

"What goofy idea are you talking about?" asked Mitzi.

"I was coming to that," replied Max. "I got in on a session with the Mother Goose-ites. Mrs. Dumpty tells their fortune from fortune cookies. Mine said, 'Depart not from the place to which fate has brought you, and you will have thrilling events unfold in your life."

"Wow!" said Mitzi. "So there you are. You'd be an idiot to leave now. Boy, I really believe in fortune cookie fortunes. You might say I *love* them." She paused a moment, and then scowled. "But you only just got here, so how were you lucky enough to get in on that?"

"I'm arriving there," said Max. He motioned Mitzi to sit on the edge of his cot wit him. And then, as her eyes grew wider and wider, he told her the whole story of seeing the goons with their shovels and lanterns, and the arrival of the Measley girls looking like two Halloween

126

ghouls. He even admitted to discovering this at the outset because he was…well, all packed and ready to take off. In for a penny, in for a pound, he decided. Mitzi just stared at him with a stony face at this piece of news.

All she said was, "Well then, go on."

So then Max went on to tell her about the Mother Goose-ites late night "stroll", and how it led finally to the invitation to meet with them the next day. When he got to the point of telling Mitzi about the map, he reached into his jeans pocket and pulled it out.

"So here it is," he said.

"You mean they trusted you with this?" she asked.

"I have it, don't I?" said Max.

"Well, how about me? Maybe they wouldn't want me to know about it," said Mitzi.

"For your information, it's fine with them," said Max. "I told them about how the Measley ghouls, I mean, excuse me, *girls,* had tried to bribe both of us, and what we intended to do about it. On top of which, they like you anyway."

"Oh, wow! Oh, wow!" she breathed. "So, okay, open it up and let's have a look at it."

Map unfolded the map, and they both poured over it.

"Hard to tell because it's so old," Max said, "There are several suspicious marks, but the one that looks most suspicious to me is about where the cemetery is. I think, anyway, as I've never been there. But I figured Digger and Dork and shovels, etc. etc."

Mitzi shuddered. "You don't need to paint a picture. I get it."

"And," continued Max, "you *did* say something about *spooky,* didn't you?"

"Yeah," said Mitzi, "only I didn't mean the cemetery. I had another place in mind. But you may be guessing right about the cemetery. So are you ready to take off?"

"Would it be okay if we took Moxie and Mojo?" Max asked. "Moose says they love playing there."

"Good idea," said Mitzi. "Then if anyone sees us, it will just look as if we're out walking the dogs."

Max hesitated. "I'll have to ask them first, but I'm sure they'll want to go. I've never heard of a dog yet that turned down a walk."

Mitzi stopped dead en route to the door.

"What do you mean 'ask them'?" said Mitzi. "Are you kidding?"

Max shrugged uncomfortably. "Well... er... a... um... I... I talk to animals, especially dogs."

"So what?" said Mitzi. "So do I."

"I...I mean I have conversations with them," said Max.

"Hmmm," hummed Mitzi without even blinking. "Okay, so let's go do it then."

They crept from the building and raced to the garage. Mojo and Moxie were in the yard behind it, leaping up onto the fence as soon as they saw Max.

"Okay, show me about this dog conversation business,"" said Mitzi.

"Moxie and Mojo, would you like to go exploring with Mitzi and me?" asked Max.

"*Yes! Yes! Yes!*" they both said, with tails wagging at full speed.

"They said 'yes'," said Max.

"What do you mean they *said* 'yes'?" said Mitzi. "I didn't hear anything. Tail wagging isn't *saying* something."

Max shrugged. "I told you. I...I talk to animals," he said.

"And I told you so do I," said Mitzi, "But they don't talk back."

"I mean I really do talk to animals," said Max. "I told you, I have conversations with them."

Mitzi just stood there, expressionless, rubbing Mojo's ears. "So how come I didn't hear anything?"

"I guess it's...it's more like I read their minds," Max said, shifting his feet uncomfortably. This is the first time he'd admitted this to anyone even himself. Mitzi would probably say he was making the whole thing up, the way Pencival did.

"That's interesting," she said at last. "*Very* interesting. Pretty cool, actually. Hmmmmm," she hummed. "Well, so shall we take off?"

Just like that!

Mitzi's reaction was equal to Moose saying, "Is that so?" For the second time ever, there was someone believing and not making fun of him!

In minutes, they had got the dog's leashes from Moose, and the four of them, Max, Mitzi, Moxie and Mojo set off into the woods.

Having the dogs with them was, without doubt, a good idea, Max soon decided. Overhanging branches and vines from the trees definitely made things shadowy and spooky. That word seemed to fit more than just the cemetery they were approaching. But there was no doubt it *really* fit the cemetery when they arrived there.

It took only a glance to see that it was very old. Most of the gravestones were moss covered and many of them were tilted. Whatever grass was there hadn't been mowed in a very long time, and it was thick with weeds.

This must have been here long before even Dolly Manor, now Measley Manor, was even thought of.

But one thing was also clear. There had been some recent serious digging going on there. There was fresh dirt around three of the larger gravestones, as if the graves has been dug up, and then probably refilled with the former contents. Why? And what exactly were they looking for?

And did they find it?

Max and Mitzi looked at one another, and they both shrugged. But neither one said anything. Who wanted to say aloud what they might both have been thinking. That maybe some millionaire a gazillion years ago might have been buried there with his big, bulging bags of money? It was too creepy, creepy, creepy!

Chapter XIX

In which Max and Mitzi go exploring further, and Moxie
and Mojo make a *very* interesting discovery.

"I say we get out of here," said Max. "The boys have done all the sniffing they need to do."

"I won't argue about that," said Mitzi. "Are you going to tell the Mother Goose-ites about this?"

Max shrugged. "I hate to, but I guess I'll have to. If I hadn't stopped them the other night, they would have discovered this for themselves.

After all, they had the map, didn't they?"

"What do you suppose they'll do about this?" asked Mitzi.

"I expect nothing. What could they do? They're practically prisoners,"

said Max. "Anyway, are we going to go exploring further? You asked me if I was afraid of spooky places. Was this one it?"

"Nope," said Mitzi. "I've never really been here before. I always just race past it on the way to the shore. There's a little sandy beach there that's mostly deserted. That's where I was going to take you."

"Sounds great!" said Max. "You hear that, boys, water! I'll bet you'll love that."

Moxie and Mojo's tails wagged furiously.

The overhanging trees didn't seem nearly so threatening to Max now that he knew that they were headed for a sandy beach and not an old cemetery where the goons had been digging up who knows what. It was a fairly long way to get there, but definitely worth the walk, thought Max. So did Moxie and Mojo, if their excited jumping around was any sign.

About thirty old, weathered rickety wood steps zigzagged down to a small sandy cove. The sun sparkled off small waves which that day were not much more than ripples. They lapped up on smooth sand dotted with black clamshells. Far off in the distance a sailboat was sailing by, not much more than a dot on the horizon.

"Wow!" thought Max.

As soon as they had climbed down the steps, he and Mitzi took off their shoes and socks, and Max took off Moxie and Mojo's leashes. Then, after playing a long game of tag with the dogs, Max and Mitzi dropped breathlessly down on the sand to watch the delighted dogs still playing in the water.

"I don't know why you said this place was spooky," Max said. "Doesn't seem very spooky to me."

"Who said this was the place I meant?" said Mitzi.

"You mean there's more?" asked Max.

"Uh huh," said Mitzi, with a mysterious smile. "Just look around yourself."

Max did, and didn't see anything that remotely fit the word.

"You got me," he said. "I give up."

"Okay," said Mitzi, "just go back to the steps, and look behind where the last ten of them make a turn."

Max scrambled up and did it. "So what?" he said. "Nothing here but a bunch of bushes."

"That's right," replied Mitzi. "Wild blueberry bushes. I was down picking berry's when I happened to push one branch aside. Do it now!"

Max did, and if there is such a thing as jaws dropping, that's what Max's jaw did.

"D...d...did you go into it?" he asked.

"About four steps," said Mitzi. "I'm not so brave...or stupid...that I'd go into a cave hidden behind bushes on a deserted beach nobody even knew I'd been visiting. But now that you're with me, what do you think?

Shall we check it out? We might find some interesting shells, or whatever."

"Sure, why not?" said cool-guy Max, whose heart had actually begun to race. Exploring a cave...wow! "But we'll have to take the boys. I can't leave them out here alone."

"Good idea!" said Mitzi.

"We should have a flashlight," Max said. "Except I don't even own one, not any more at any rate."

"I brought my mini. Don't forget," said Mitzi, "I've been here before."

"Then let's do it!" said Max.

As soon as Moxie and Mojo has been leashed, Max and Mitzi pushed the bushes aside, and started into the cave. After going just a few feet, they were in pitch darkness except for the tiny light from Mitzi's mini flashlight. The dogs for some reason started straining at their leashes.

"Look, boys," said Max. "This isn't necessary. Just where do you think you're going."

"The boys aren't telling," said Mitzi. "How far do you think we ought to go? There's two of us, but we could be falling into a deep hole."

"Okay, boys, that's enough," said Max.

But Moxie and Mojo kept on whining and pulling. Max was having trouble holding them back.

And then, all at once, they stopped and started sniff, sniff, sniffing at a crack in the cave wall. Then they both began to whine and scratch at the wall.

"Do you suppose it's some dead sea creature got caught in there," said Mitzi.

"Is that what it is, you two?" asked Max.

"Yes, and no," said Moxie and Mojo. "But there might be something else."

"They think there's something else," said Max. "Come on, flash your light on the wall and I'll help them dig."

The wall was crumbly, and in moments, Max pulled out the empty shell of some kind of sea creature, just as Mitzi suspected. This was disappointing, but what did they expect?

"Probably an old crab that got lost," Mitzi said.

But Max saw something else there as well.

"We told you!" said the dogs.

What they had found besides the empty shell was a cord of some kind. Max pulled on it, and nearly fell backward when with a sudden swoosh, out came the whole cord attached to a dark sack, stained and filthy. Both the cord and sack appeared to be leather.

"Wow!" said Mitzi under her breath. "What in heck is that? I...I hope it's not got something in it...well, sort of like...old bones!"

Max was thinking the same thing. They probably both had cemeteries and shovels on their minds. But then it could be just a bunch of crab shells from formerly dead crabs like Mitzi's first thought.

"Should we open it?" she asked.

"Well, yeah, naturally," said Max. "It...it would be loony not to."

He began to tug at the cord while the dogs danced excitedly around him. All at once, he almost toppled backwards, catching himself just in time as the cord snapped off the sack. He righted himself, took a deep breath, and pulled on the cord. It broke off in his hand.

Then, after a long look at Mitzi, he took both hands, pulled the sack open, and peered into it.

"Is it o...o...old bones?" asked Mitzi, shuddering.

"No way!" said Max. "Here, take a look."

Mitzi looked. "Omigosh!" she breathed

What the two of them were looking at with popping eyes was gold coins. A whole, great sack of them!

"These look really old," said Max. "Probably gold doubloons, or something like that. I mean, I have no idea what gold doubloons look like, but they must be something like this."

"Do you suppose this is what the Measley witches have been looking for?" Mitzi said.

"Who knows," replied Max. "I wouldn't be surprised." He dug the map out of his jeans pocket and unfolded it. "Mitzi, shine your flashlight on this."

The tiny light moving around the map found what they had thought might be an X where the cemetery was. On second thought, maybe it was just a symbol of some kind. But looking further at the point where the cove might be was a genuine X. It was where the map was creased from being folded, and thus was easily missed.

"Wow!" said Max. "This definitely must be what the Measley's are looking for. But how do you suppose they even knew there was such a thing as a map?"

"I'll bet they didn't," said Mitzi. "I think they've just been guessing. But Mum told me she'd heard this was once a smuggler's cove, and there were rumors that they'd hid their loot somewhere around here. But she was sure it was all just native gossip."

"Whew!" breathed Max. "I wonder how the Measley girls heard about it. They must have, and then just got a good deal no doubt stealing Measley Manor from the Dolly's at some stupid low price. I'm just surprised they didn't go nosing around here."

Mitzi giggled. "Wild blackberry bushes is probably why! So they've been trying the cemetery. Who looks behind bushes? Anyway, so now we've found the doubloons, what are we going to do about it? If Measley Manor actually includes all the land down to the sea, don't these doubloons really belong to the Measley's whether we like it or not? Are we going to have to tell them about it?"

"What do you think, fellows?" Max asked Moxie and Mojo. "Do we have to tell the Measley's?"

"Absolutely not!" they both replied. "Who you have to tell is the Mother Goose-ites. See what they have to say."

Max repeated this to Mitzi.

"So what do *they* think we ought to do with all the doubloons?" asked Mitzi.

"You heard that, you two," said Max. "What *should* we do with them?"

"Too risky carrying the sack back. First, take one of the doubloons and stick it in your jeans pocket so you'll have proof to show them" advised Moxie. "Then you'd better pack the rest of the doubloons in their sack right back where you found them."

"*Absolutely!*" agreed Mojo.

"I have a good idea," said Moxie. "Take one of these things and leave it at the cemetery where the goons have been digging. Get them all excited thinking they've found the Measley Manor treasure!"

Max passed all this on to Mitzi, who thought planting a gold doubloon in the cemetery was the greatest idea yet. She just grinned as Max took one of the doubloons and stuck it in his jeans pocket along with the map.

It wasn't easy, though, trying to shove the sack back into the wall, and then packing sand and rocks against it to look as if it was the way they'd found it. The dogs, of course, were very excited about this whole event. But Mitzi and Max finally decided they'd done the best they could. They also remembered to fix up the blackberry bushes so it looked as if they hadn't been touched. After that they raced back to Measley Manor,

136

stopping only to place a gold coin on one of the cemetery gravesite where nobody but a blind idiot could miss it.

"When are you going to see the Mother Goose-ites about this?" asked Mitzi.

"Probably this evening after their dinner hour," replied Max. "The sooner the better!"

"As long as you haven't decided to run away first," said Mitzi, grinning.

"Oh, shut up!" said Max.

Those plans were certainly now on hold until the matter of the gold doubloons had been settled. But what if he showed up at Mr. Fitzbottom's desk with those in his pocket, who knew where that might lead. All this, of course, was if he decided to run away. And that had now definitely become a very big IF!

Chapter XX

In which Max has to do a good acting job with the Measley's, then consults with Mrs. Dumpty and is asked a surprising question about Moose.

Max was tiptoeing down the hall toward Mrs. Dumpty's room that evening, and never heard the silent footsteps coming up behind him.

"And what, may we ask," said Ruby Measley, "is the reason for tiptoeing down the hall, young man, at this hour? We trust you are not up to mischief?"

"Oh...oh...oh, no!" said Max, whispering, and at the same time thinking fast. "I...I...I'm practicing...my spying techniques!" He was quickly getting very good at out-Measley-ing the Measley girls!

"Splendid!" said Ruby. Then she turned to her twin. "We were quite right, Pearl, to allow Moose to bring this boy here."

"We were, indeed, sister dear," replied Pearl. "So go along now, boy, and we hope you will soon have something interesting to report to us."

"You...you haven't in your spying duties heard anything about a kind of...of a map, have you?" asked

Ruby, with a raised-eyebrow glance at her twin. "I believe we may have mentioned this subject to you before."

Max frowned as if thinking deeply.

"No," he said, chewing on his lip. "But there are scraps of paper in the waste bins. Do you think I should check all those?"

"What an excellent idea!" said Pearl. "You are a clever young man, indeed. You will go far at Measley Manor, don't you think, sister?"

"Oh yes!" said Ruby. "But we mustn't keep you from your duties. So run along now," she paused to give Max a sly smile, "I mean tiptoe along, of course!"

They turned to wave at Max as they drifted silently down the hall. Max kept on tiptoeing right past Mrs. Dumpty's door. But as soon as the Measley's had disappeared, he turned swiftly back, and knocked.

"I'm sorry," said Mrs. Dumpty's voice from behind the door. "But I'm in my robe. Could you return later? Who is it, please?"

"The Measley's are out prowling the halls. I...I have something important to show you," said Max.

The door flew open at once. Mrs. Dumpty wasn't in her robe at all, but dressed in her slacks and a bright turquoise shirt. And she wasn't alone.

"It's okay!" she said in the direction of her closet, whose doors were closed.

The closet doors opened, and out came Ms. Bo Peep and Police Officer Dickory.

"Darlin'," said Mrs. Dumpty, "Ms. Bo Peep had something important to tell me as well, and she brought Officer Dickory along so we could have a conference and decide what to do about it. But let's hear what you have to tell us."

"Well," said Max, "you know that Mitzi and I were going exploring and had the old map with us. What we found was that there was some very suspicious digging going on around some of the graves in the cemetery. The

Measley's and the goons were definitely looking for something."

"As we all suspected, darlin'," said Mrs. Dumpty.

"Mitzi and I and Moxie and Mojo, who we had with us, didn't hang around there for long. We went on down to the cove that I didn't even know was there. Well, I thought the cemetery was the spooky place Mitzi had told me about. But seems it was a place at the cove. It was a cave Mitzi discovered hidden behind some wild blackberry bushes under those rickety old stairs. So we went in. Moxie and Mojo were getting all excited about something hidden behind a crack in the wall. So we dug behind there and found this old sack. And in the sack, we found a pile of these." Max reached into his jeans pocket and pulled out a gold coin. "I thought it might be a gold doubloon."

The three Goose-ites gasped.

"Here, let me have a look at it," said Officer Dickory. He took the coin from Max and turned it back and forth in his hands. "I'm no expert, but I'd guess that's what this is. Mrs. Muffet probably would have a better idea."

"Mercy!" said Mrs. Dumpty

"Mercy, indeed!" said Officer Dickory. "Even a small sack full of these must be worth a fortune. So where's the sack now?"

"We decided to hide it right back where we found it," said Max and then hesitated, "I...I mean, the dogs decided it for us."

"How did they do that, darlin'?"' asked Mrs. Dumpty.

"I...I asked them," said Max. "I...I can talk to animals."

"Why aren't I surprised?" said Mrs. Dumpty, giving a knowing look at Ms. Bo Peep and Officer Dickory.

"Mitzi wondered if we had to tell the Measley's about this as the cave might be on the Measley Manor property," said Max. "But the dogs said we should tell you first."

"Those are two smart dogs," said Officer Dickory, and then added, "Which we've all known!"

"I'm not sure if it was Moxie or Mojo," said Max. "But one of them suggested we put a coin on one of the gravesites in the cemetery where the goons had been digging to throw them off."

"Smarter and smarter," said Officer Dickory. "Brilliant! I assume you did just that?"

"Oh sure!" said Max. "But are we going to have to tell the Measley's about this? I mean, if we found the stuff on their land and all that?"

The three Mother Goose-ites exchanged narrow-eyed glances.

"The question is, Max," said Officer Dickory, "what is and isn't their land. This is something we have to find out."

"And to add to all this, darlin'," said Mrs. Dumpty, "you remember I said Ms. Bo Peep had something important to tell us."

Max nodded.

"Tell Max what you think you may have found out, Peeps," said Mrs. Dumpty.

"Remember what I was doing when you came into my room, Max?" asked Ms. Bo Peep.

"Looked to me as if you were studying fingerprints," said Max.

"Exactly!" said Ms. Bo Peep. "Used to be part of my profession as a detective, and now it's a hobby. But when I came here, which was when it was still Dolly Manor, I also brought some files with me, nothing to do with fingerprints. Several of them contained old newspaper clippings I'd hung on to, not really thinking they'd be of any use as I was out of the detecting business. I was going through them just last night thinking I might as well get rid of them, when one of the pictures caught my eye. It was of a group of ten people, and four of them looked vaguely familiar. I picked up my magnifying glass and took a closer look. Then I took an even closer look, and decided to have a meeting with Officer Dickory and Mrs. Dumpty."

"Show him the picture, Peeps," said Mrs. Dumpty. "He's probably got better eyesight than the three of us put together. And read what it says under the picture, darlin'."

Ms. Bo Peep handed Max the yellowed newspaper clipping she'd been holding, along with her large magnifying glass.

Max read the caption under the picture, and then at the picture itself.

"Four of them..." Max looked closer, "look sort of like..."

"Sort of?" asked Ms. Bo Peep.

"Well, it's more *exactly* like..." said Max.

"Bingo!" said Ms. Bo Peep. "And don't even breathe the word. We all know it, and that's what the three of us think."

"Wow!" said Max.

"Wow, indeed, darlin'," said Mrs. Dumpty. "So go on, Peeps."

"The problem is, I can't really go on," said Ms. Bo Peep. "Our private telephones have been removed, and the only one in the hall for us all to use we believe is bugged. They even took our computers away from those of us who had them. We are totally incommunicado, so to speak. Do you understand what that means, young man?"

"Sure," said Max. "It means there's no way you can reach anyone you need to reach to tell them about this."

"Bingo again!" said Ms. Bo Peep.

"So I guess we can't call anyone about the doubloons either, can we?"
asked Max.

"Well, there *is* one person we could talk to about it," said Mrs. Dumpty.

"I think we should talk to Moose and see what he thinks."

"Moose? But...but," Max stammered, "Moose isn't...well, Moose is just a handyman. How...how would *he* know what to do?"

"Is that what you think?" asked Mrs. Dumpty. "Just a handyman? Exactly how much do you know about your cousin Moose, darlin'?"

Max shrugged. "I guess not much except he's a handyman who probably only graduated from kindergarten or grade school. I...I'm not even sure he's my cousin, or anything else."

The three *Mother Goose-ites* all exchanged glances and shook their heads.

"Darlin'," said Mrs. Dumpty, "I think you need a serious talk with Moose.

Tell him what you think, and then I think you should believe what he tells you."

"Should...should I tell him about the doubloons?" asked Max.

"Absolutely!" said Officer Dickory. "And tell him Mrs. Dumpty and Ms. Bo Peep and I urgently need to consult with him."

"Will you do that, darlin'?" asked Mrs. Dumpty.

Max nodded. That was about all he was capable of doing at that moment.

Chapter XXI

In which Max makes his report to Moose.

"**S**o what is there about Moose that I don't know?" Max asked Moxie and Mojo that night when Moose had happily invited him for his favorite broccoli pizza.

"*Beats us,*" said Moxie.

"You'll have to ask him yourself," said Mojo.

Max already knew he'd have to do that. He was beginning to admit to himself that the only things Sir Launcelot and Lady Guinevere had said to him, and now Moxie and Mojo, were things he already knew, or wanted to hear. Pencival had said that if he believed he talked to animals, and more especially that they talked back to him, that he was loony. He knew his parents only pretended to believe it. But Moose didn't question it. Neither did Mitzi. Was he just imagining that he could talk to animals? Did it matter as long as *he* believed it?

Anyway, he decided to wait until he and Moose had finished their dinner of pizza with broccoli (again, but Max didn't mind), watching the evening news on television as they ate before saying anything to him.

Then, as soon as Moose had settled himself into his chair and picked up his book, Max went and stood in front of him.

"What is it, kid?" Moose asked. "Got something on your mind?"

"Yes, this," said Max, and held out the gold coin.

Moose took it from him and flipped it back and forth in his fingers. Then he gave a low whistle.

"Where did *this* come from?" he asked.

"Mitzi and I found a whole sack of them in the cave down by the shore that Mitzi discovered once. It's behind the wild blackberry bushes under the old stairwell. Well, it was more like Moxie and Mojo found the sack," said Max. "They were digging in the wall because they must have smelled some kind of sea creature that had died there, a crab or something. Or that's what we thought anyway. Then we realized that the cave was marked on the map with an X."

"The plot seems to be thickening," said Moose. "What map are we talking about?"

"It's one Mrs. Dumpty found in her closet," Max replied. "The Mother Goose-ites all said it was okay for me to have it, because I told the Measley's I'd spy for them, which I only did so I could tell them fairy tales about what I found out and..."

"Whoah! Whoah! Whoah, there, Max!" said Moose, holding up a hand. "You're getting way ahead of me. First of all, you've been here a couple of weeks or so and you're already on the in track with the Mother Goose-ites, as you call them. Would you like to explain how that happened? Take your time. I'm listening."

Max looked down and studied the toes of his shoes. "I...I...I told Mrs. Dumpty my story, and...and...and she said she'd be my grandmother, and...and...I sort of cried. Not a lot. Just...just...just a little. I...

I...I *never* cry!"

146

"I do," said Moose. "Crying is okay. And heaven knows you have a right to cry buckets, Max. Forget about it. Anyway, so go on."

"Well," Max began, "one night I saw Digger and Dork leaving the building with shovels and lanterns, and later the Measley's showed up. They went off somewhere together. Then the next night I saw the Mother Goose-ites all going in same direction with their flashlights. I ran out and warned them that Digger and Dork and the Measley's might be showing up. So they came right back in, and then Mrs. Dumpty invited me to a meeting in her room the next day. They have these meetings, Moose, where she tells their fortunes from fortune cookies. It's really neat."

"Fortune cookie fortunes, eh? They've never invited me to have my fortune told. I should feel insulted." Moss said, grinning. "You really seem to have won them over, Max. But what, I'd like to know, ever happened to wrinkled old people who give you the creeps?"

"I guess they're sort of still wrinkled old people," Max said uncomfortably, "But...but...but I guess they...they...they don't give me the creeps anymore."

"Glad to hear that," said Moose. "But we've strayed way off the subject. Let's go back to the map and the gold coins. By the way, though how come it wasn't just you, but you and Mitzi who went exploring. I had the feeling you two were more or less at each other's throats when you met."

"Oh," said Max indifferently, "she's okay. She's...she's pretty cool, and all that. We've sort of become friends."

"I'm glad you two have teamed up," Moose said. "You're right, she's a cool kid. But was it okay with the...um...er...Mother Goose-ites for her to know about the map?"

"Oh sure!" said Max. "I mean, they know the Measley's have tried to get her to spy as well as me. She told them she would, but she's not going to. I gave her the idea of feeding them a bunch of junk, though." Max tried to look modest, but probably wasn't too successful.

"I'll bet you did!" said Moose, grinning again. "So let's go on about the map and the gold coins. Why did you decide to come to me with this?"

"Because the Mother Goose-ites wanted me to tell you about it. They say they urgently need to consult with you. I'm not sure why," said Max. "Maybe they've never told you about the fortune cookie fortunes, but I...I...I think they really like you and trust you."

"Good to know," Moose said. "The feeling is mutual. I'll make it a point to see Mrs. Dumpty as soon as possible."

"But please be careful, Moose," said Max. "Those Measley's come creeping around and you never know where they are or when they'll be there."

"Don't worry," said Moose. "I'm on to the two of them. Just *you* be careful as well, kid. They can be *very* persuasive. Now, is there anything else you want to tell me?"

"Sort...sort...sort of," said Max, not quite able to look Moose in the eye.

"Well then, out with it," said Moose, stretching his legs ahead of him comfortably. "I'm listening."

Max ran over to the bookcase, pulled out the folder that held the large piece of paper he had accidentally spilled. Then he took it over to Moose and handed it to him.

"I...I...I guess I thought this was a fake. I mean, you being a handyman and all that. But...but...but could you explain it? Mrs. Dumpty said I was to ask you, and I was to believe everything you told me."

"And will you?" asked Moose.

"Sure," said Max.

And meant it.

 # Chapter XXII

In which Max learns this lesson from Moose: that while skimmed milk can often masquerade as cream, the reverse can be just as true, that cream can masquerade as skimmed milk.

"**I** wasn't snooping, Moose, honest," said Max. "It just fell out of the folder on the shelf I knocked into accidentally."

"No apologies necessary," said Moose. "But what it is you wanted to know about it?"

"I didn't look at it very carefully," said Max. "But I what I saw I figured was probably a fake."

"Because I'm just working here as a handyman living off a garage?" asked Moose.

Max nodded slowly.

"And you figured I was probably lucky to graduate from grade school?"

Max nodded again. He didn't think he'd better mention graduating from kindergarten.

"Can't say I blame you," said Moose. "But you *do* know what this is, don't you?"

Max nodded a third time.

"And though I suppose it could be done, wouldn't you know it could be a pretty hard thing to fake?"

"I guess so," said Max. "But if it's true, what *are* you doing here? I mean, who graduates from a university with a law degree and gets a job as a handyman in a home for old people?"

"And you might ask who passes the bar, gets a job with a top law firm at an enormous salary, and ends up at Measley Manor? I don't blame you for wondering about it, Max," Moose said. "I sometimes wonder about it myself, until I go back to the reason for it. Then I stop wondering."

"So what's the reason?" Max asked.

"The reason," said Moose, "is that I had a tragedy in my life just as you did. My wife, Peggy, and I had been sweethearts since we were in first grade. When she died having a baby who might have been not much older than you if he'd lived, I lost interest in law and the company I was with. So I just chucked it all and for a couple of years signed on as a seaman on a freighter. If you look further in that file folder, you'll see my papers for that as well."

"But how did you end up here?" asked Max.

"Just saw an ad in a paper and applied for the job," Moose replied. "It was Dolly Manor then. Shortly after I signed up, Martin and Mary Dolly had to sell the place. Seems they weren't very good managers and were ready to lose it anyway. I'm not sure I would have joined up if I'd had an interview with the Measley girls."

"So why are you staying?" Max asked. "Can't you just leave?"

"Sure," said Moose. "But I've fallen for all your Mother Goose-ites, just as I believe you have. I think the Measley's are doing everything they can to make their lives miserable. The fact they aren't entirely succeeding just shows what kind of spirit these lovely old people have. Anyway, I'm sticking around, with the crazy idea that maybe my law degree might come in handy one of

150

these days. Don't ask me how. But I'm not going to desert them. And that's the whole story, Max."

Suddenly, Max found himself grinning.

"So what's so funny?" Moose asked.

"What's so funny," said Max, "is that you sticking around with your law degree might not be so crazy after all. Mrs. Dumpty, Ms. Bo Peep, and Officer Dickory have told me to tell you that they want to meet with you right away. They have something very interesting to show you."

"And I suppose you know what it is?' said Moose.

"I just might," said Max.

"Is it something to do with the gold coins?" asked Moose.

"That's just part of it," said Max.

"And I suppose you're not going to tell me the rest?" said Moose.

"Nope!" said Max. "I think they'd better do it. But please, whatever you do, don't let the Measley's know."

"Look, I may be a mere guy with a law degree, and not a Ballyhoo boy, Max, but I think I'm smart enough not to go running to the Measley's unless the building is burning down," said Moose. "And even that's not a dead certainty."

"Sorry about that," said Max.

"You know something?" said Moose. "I was thinking I should have had my head examined for taking you in, cousin. But I'm beginning to have the feeling it was really a very brilliant move on my part."

"I think it was brilliant that I decided to stick around," said Max.

"What's that supposed to mean?" asked Moose.

"Oh, nothing," said Max.

There seemed no point in telling Moose about the roller coaster. A roller coaster just about permanently stalled was hardly worth mentioning. But seems as if he'd probably guessed about it anyway.

"And he even talks to animals!" said Moose.

"That, too," said Max, grinning.

 # Chapter XXIII

In which Max takes a part in a scene more interesting
than anything he ever read in a book at ballyhoo but
which, in the end, might mean another dose of bad news
and another case of things ganging aft agley.

"**Y**oung man! Young man!"

Max recognized the voices hissing down the hall at him. He came to an instant stop, and whirled around.

"You haven't been reporting to us," said Miss Ruby Measley, giving Max a sly smile.

"You haven't found out anything...er...*interesting*?" asked Miss Pearl. "Have you, naughty boy?" she added, pursing her lips coyly.

"Well, Mitzi and I were going to report something later," said Max, widening his eyes innocently as he told a big, fat lie. "Snitch didn't come in today, so I thought I'd take care of toilets and trash first before I did anything else."

"Yes! Yes! Yes!" said the two of them excitedly. "Toilets and trash first. Of course! Of course! Good boy! Toilets and trash must always come first. But tell us what you've found out. Come! Come! Out with it!" Max could practically see the drool running down their chins.

"But Pearl," said Ruby. "This isn't the best place to talk. The walls have eyes and ears, don't you know."

"I do indeed, Ruby," replied Pearl. "Perhaps Max and Mitzi would like to visit us this afternoon and we can have a nice cozy chat over tea...that is, *milk* and cookies. Would you like that, Max, dear boy?"

Now, after Moose had had his meeting with the Mother Goose-ites, he had warned Max to stay clear of the Measley girls. He was going to make at least two trips into the city, and didn't want Max being quizzed about it.

"Is it about the doubloons and picture in the newspaper?" Max had asked.

"Ask me no questions, I'll tell you no lies, Max," said Moose. "And you're better off not knowing in case the Measley's start quizzing you. I'm telling them I need to get special parts for various repair projects about here and I can do it best in the city. 'Parts', Max. Just remember 'parts'."

Max hoped against hopes that there wasn't going to be any quizzing, and he wouldn't be bumping into the Measley's any time soon. And he would certainly rather choke than go to their rooms for milk and cookies. He had no plans for going there any time within the next millennium, or ever, but he at least now had come up with the sudden idea of coming with Mitzi so he wouldn't be alone with them. He only hoped he could find Mitzi and persuade her to go along with him.

As soon as the Measley's were out of sight, Max raced up to the kitchen, and he was in luck. Mitzi was there, and fortunately Mrs. Fiddle had stepped out at that moment.

"Mitzi, we're stuck," Max whispered. "I stupidly told the Measley's you and I had something to report to them, and now we've been invited to their rooms for milk and cookies to do it. You'll come won't you?"

"Why not?" said Mitzi coolly.

154

"Thanks!" said Max. "But what are we going to say to them?"

"No problem," said Mitzi.

"But whatever we do, in case they ask, we can't say anything about Moose's trip to the city either," said Max. "He wouldn't even really tell me why he was going, but I think it has something to do with the map and the coins, and a newspaper picture I haven't told you about yet. All I know is that he was all dolled up in a coat and tie and didn't even look like Moose. But if the Measley's ask, we don't know anything. Got it?"

"Got it!" said Mitzi.

When the two of them knocked on the door of the Measley's rooms late that afternoon, they were all prepared with exactly what each of them was going to report as a result of their spying missions.

"Well, well, well, out with it!" said Ruby, her eyes gleaming. "No milk and cookies before your reports, you know."

With this, Max and Mitzi exchanged telling glances. Max knew that he and Mitzi would both agree as to what the Measley's could do with their milk and cookies!

"Mitzi, suppose you go first," said Pearl.

Mitzi frowned, pretending to go into deep thought.

"Well," said Mitzi at last, "Dr. Humpty thinks he's discovered a new planet. He doesn't want anyone to know about it just yet, though. But I promised I'd let you know anything I found out, so is this something important?"

Mitzi ended this with a wide-eyed, innocent stare. It was all Max could do not to grin when he saw the identical looks of dismay on the Measley twin faces.

"Thank you, Mitzi," said Ruby, who finally somehow managed a sour smile. "That is not quite what we had in mind, but it is certainly a start. Perhaps Max can do better."

"Oh, I think I can," said Max promptly. "Commander King Cole told me secretly that he is planning to find someone to build a sailboat for him." He paused to see how this was going over. Then he added, "He intends to sail around the world in it." He paused again, and then concluded triumphantly, "Alone!"

The looks on the Measley faces could hardly be described, but Mitzi had to throw her hands to her face to choke back giggles, pretending to keep back a coughing fit. Max was having an equally hard time controlling his own face.

"You're sure neither of you learned anything about...er...maps, old papers, or things such as that?" asked Ruby.

Max and Mitzi exchanged innocent looks, and then both shook their heads.

"But we'll keep our eyes peeled, won't we, Mitzi?" said Max.

"And our ears, too," said Mitzi.

"Well, that will be splendid," said Ruby. "But I have another question for Max. Moose has been having to go into the city. He tells us it's for purchasing items for the workshop. Now we don't expect you to go telling tales about your cousin, but is that really why he is traveling to the city?"

"It's for parts," said Max promptly. Then he decided to get creative. "I think some are for toilets."

"Toilet parts?" said Pearl. "Why would he need those?"

"No idea, Ms. Measley," said Max, shaking his head. "I don't fix them. I only clean them."

"Of course you do," said Ruby. "But you're certain that..."

Whatever Ruby was going to say never got said. There was a loud knock on the door. She paused in mid-sentence as Pearl went to answer it. In the doorway stood Moose, complete with an unfamiliar coat and, and two men also in neat dark coats and ties. Moose frowned when he saw Max and Mitzi in the room.

"I...I...was just telling the Miss Measley's that...that you'd gone into the city to buy parts," Max blurted out.

156

Moose's frown instantly turned into a broad smile. "Of course!" he said. "And that's exactly correct, Max. But while I was back in town, I had to stop at the bank. While waiting in line, I met these two gentlemen and they wondered if I could direct them to Measley Manor. We began to talk while waiting in line, and when I revealed that I was employed here, they revealed to me that they had an interesting proposition to make to the owners. When we were finished with our business, I had them follow me here in their car."

Ruby and Pearl exchanged glances.

"An interesting proposition, did you say?" asked Ruby.

"Yes, *very* interesting," said one of the men, raising an eyebrow. "And rewarding as well."

"Allow us to introduce ourselves," said the second man, "I'm Mr. Jones, and my friend here is Mr. Brown. We're owners of the...er...ah...investment firm of Jones and Brown. If you two ladies would accompany us to our car," said the second man, "we'd like you do us the honor of dining with us at a restaurant of your choice in town to discuss the matter."

Ruby and Pearl exchanged further glances. They were clearly bursting with curiosity, excitement, and greed.

"That would be splendid, indeed! Would it not?" gushed Ruby.

"Oh yes, yes, yes!" agreed her twin eagerly.

"We shall be ready in a moment," said Pearl. Then she waved a hand airily at Moose. "You may go now, and please take the children with you."

Moments later, Moose, Max, and Mitzi were in the hall. But silently Moose motioned them to follow him downstairs to the lobby. There he had the three of them stand hidden behind the door leading to the dining room.

"What are we doing here, Moose?" Max whispered.

"Just watching," replied Moose. "I want to be sure the Measley girls leave the building. Quiet! Here they come now!"

In moments, the Measley twins, tittering and gushing for all their worth, had been escorted from the building by Mr. Jones and Mr. Brown.

Moose turned and gave Max and Mitzi a big grin. "Mr. Jones and Mr. Brown, kids, are alias plain clothes officers O'Toole and McDougal. Ruby and Pearl will unfortunately not be dining at the restaurant of their choice, but will be booked and then have the finest meal offered at the local city jail. Capturing these two after all these years will be quite a coup for our local cops. Furthermore, back-up officers will be picking up those two thugs working for the girls. They had some connection with that gang of thieves as well, it seems."

"So were those pictures in the newspaper clipping who the Mother Goose-ites and I thought they were?" asked Max.

"Dead on!" said Moose. "They were much younger, of course, but they were the only two of a smuggling gang, who also had a couple of murders on their hands, who escaped and were never caught. Then I checked with some pals at the F.B.I. from my law days, and the fingerprints Ms. Bo Peep lifted proved it without a doubt."

"But why did they want Dolly Manor?" asked Max.

"I suspect they may have heard the cove where you and Mitzi found the coins had once been used by smugglers. After that it was just guessing, which let them to the cemetery. But they without much doubt may have had in mind another smuggling racket. Don't know if they knew for a fact about the gold coins, or just guessed, and guessed about the map. They probably had plenty of money from their smuggling days to buy Dolly Manor and whatever they might find with it."

Moose paused a moment, and then shook his head sadly. "They have no more interest in the welfare of the Mother Goose-ites than taking a trip to the moon. They were just hoping to find gold here, and use the dear people as a cover for a smuggling operation." Then Moose grinned. "Mr. Jones and Mr. Brown may be just frosting on their cake, or so they think tomorrow morning, we'll knock on every Goose-ite door and tell the gang to meet in the lobby at noon tomorrow. If asked, just say not to worry, you believe it's only to take a vote on something. This is true, as we're all going to have to decide on the future of Measley Manor when the Measley's are out of the picture. But right now, Max and Mitzi, we're taking Moxie and Mojo, and the five of us are going on a treasure hunt!"

The Measley's off to jail! Digger and Dork with them! Going on a treasure hunt! This was all terrifically exciting. What might Max have missed if he'd run away? Wow!

But on the other hand...

Could the future of Measley Manor, of Moose and Mitzi and the Mother Goose-ites now all be in jeopardy? Was he, Max, doomed to go on losing one family after another? And where was he to go next if Moose decided to abandon him? Was he going to end up like Oliver Twist in some kind of orphanage? Well, at one time hadn't he had thought an orphanage was better than where he was? But that was then. This was now.

Besides, it's one thing to go someplace when it's your own idea to do it. It's another to be sent someplace when it's somebody else's idea because they haven't got a better one.

Alas, for Max, things were quite possibly ganging aft agley all over again!

Chapter XXIV

In which Max learns some startling news that he never, never, never, never, *never* ever expected to hear.

t exactly twelve noon the next day they were all gathered in the lobby of Measley Manor. The "they" were all the Mother Goose-ites:

Mrs. Dumpty
Commander King Cole
Ms. Bo Peep
Coach Winkie
Mrs. Muffet
Dr. Humpty
Mrs. Diddle
Officer Dickory
Dr. Doodle
Mr. Tweedle-dee
Besides the Mother Goose-ites, there were also:
Moose
Max
Mitzi
Mrs. Fiddle
Moxie

Mojo

Snitch

Snitch had reappeared with a big bruise on his cheeks. When Max asked him about it, he told Max he'd fallen off the steps at home, and to mind his own business. So Max did, but he couldn't help feeling sorry for Snitch anyway.

Whatever decisions were going to be made, it seems that one already *had* been. Dogs (properly leashed, of course!) were now allowed back in Measley Manor! The Mother Goose-ites were so busy with ear rubbing and back scratching the delighted dogs as Max led them around, they seemed to have forgotten that dogs were no longer allowed in the building. And then somebody remembered that they were supposed to be having a meeting about something, and it probably would involve the Measley's. But where were they? Why hadn't they yet arrived?

Then at last, Moose got up in front of them all and said, "Well I guess our meeting had better come to order, and we'll get to the business of the day."

Mrs. Dumpty raised her hand hesitantly. "Shouldn't...shouldn't we wait for the Measley's?" she asked.

"Probably not. They...er...um...are probably not in a position to come," said Moose, clearly trying to keep a straight face. "But I'm here with some good news and some possibly not-so-good news. Which would you all like first?"

Commander King Cole raised his hand. "Why don't we get the good news first so we can have something to be happy about when we get the not-so-good news? Does everyone agree with that philosophy?" The Mother Goose-ites all showed their agreement by clapping.

"Well," said Moose, "first of all, I understand that all of you here, Mrs. Fiddle and Snitch excepted, knew about a certain map found by Mrs. Dumpty. Is that correct?"

162

Everyone but Mrs. Fiddle and Snitch, nodded.

"And," continued Moose, "were you all told about the gold coins that were then found by Max and Mitzi with the help of Moxie and Mojo?"

Everyone but Mrs. Fiddle and Snitch, nodded again.

"And did Mrs. Dumpty, Officer Dickory, and Ms. Bo Peep, tell you about the picture from an old newspaper, and the fingerprints that Ms. Bo Peep collected?" Moose asked.

Once again, all but Mrs. Fiddle and Snitch nodded.

"Okay then," said Moose, "I am happy to report to you that my trip into the city confirmed everyone's suspicions. The Measley twins were indeed once members of a notorious band of smugglers and murderers, but happened never to have been captured with the rest. And I am also happy to report to you that they went off in the capable hands of a Mr. Jones and Mr. Brown, alias plain clothes officers O'Toole and McDougal, and are probably behind bars at this very moment. Digger and Dork were also part of that gang, and they're being properly disposed of as well."

This announcement was greeted by a stunned silence.

"Do...do...do you mean they're actually gone?" asked Mrs. Dumpty.

"That's exactly what I mean, Mrs. Dumpty," said Moose, with a big smile.

"And...and...and not coming back?" asked Mrs. Diddle.

"I very much doubt it," replied Moose.

This was almost impossible for the Mother Goose-ites to believe, but when it finally dawned on them that this news was real, the room was lit up with smiles.

"So what's the not-so-good news?" Commander King Cole asked.

Moose shrugged and grimaced. "The not-so-good news is the question of what's to become of Measley

Manor. It may be confiscated by the government and sold, to whom and for what purpose is anybody's guess."

"You mean we might all lose our homes here?" asked Dr. Doodle.

"It's possible," said Moose.

The room suddenly became very still. This really was terrible news.

"What if we were all to buy it?" asked Commander King Cole. "Could we do that?"

"I don't see how," said Moose. "All of you live off the income from your savings. You have to hang on to them."

There was silence in the room again. And then suddenly Max had an idea.

"Moose what...what...what about the gold coins? We found them. They're ours, aren't they? Couldn't we use those?"

Smiles broke out in the room again. Several of the Mother Goose-ites began to clap. But Moose shook his head.

"We could, but even though they're probably worth a great deal, I'm afraid even those coins aren't enough to buy Measley Manor. I'm going to look into it, though."

But Moose didn't sound too encouraging, and once again gloom took over the room.

And then, as they all sat there in dismal silence, the doorbell rang.

"I'll get it," said Officer Dickory, who was sitting closest to the door.

He opened the door, and a man walked in.

"I'm looking for Maximilian Pettigrew Westmorington Bassford Thorndike Finstersill Smith the Fifth," he said.

"I don't believe there's anyone here by that name," said Officer Dickory.

"Are you sure you've come to the right address?"

"Actually, yes, he has," said Moose, and quickly crossed the room.

Max, in the meantime, couldn't decide whether to stay, disappear, or just faint dead away. The man was no other than Mr. Fitzbottom!

"What can I do for you, Mr. Fitzbottom," said Moose. "If you're here to check up on Max...er...Maximilian, as you can see he's here still, alive and well."

"It wasn't so much checking up on him," said Mr. Fitzbottom, "but I do have something important to say to him."

Moose motioned to Max, who slowly crossed the room, dragging his feet.

All Mr. Fitzbottom had ever had for him was bad news, and with all that was happening, he didn't need any more. But when he arrived at the front door, Mr. Fitzbottom opened up a large brown envelope he was holding, pulled a letter from it, and handed it to him.

"Read it, young man," said Mr. Fitzbottom.

Max did. But it didn't make much sense to him. It had something to do with some very large amounts of money, but as he was now pretty much penniless except for some pocket change left over from the collection taken up for him by Mr. Fitzbottom's office, he couldn't see what all this money had to do with *him.* Was somebody expecting him to pay this? Were they being funny?

"What is this supposed to mean?" said Max, when he had finished reading.

"It means," said Mr. Fitzbottom, his pudgy face wreathed in smiles, "that your father had done a very fine job of hiding something that he somehow never managed to reveal to anybody. It was locked up in a vault in a bank that somehow or other only one person knew about, and that person was no longer there. This was discovered quite accidentally, but it seems your father left you a pile of money that can't be touched by anyone but you."

A "pile"! There was one after all! An *ENORMOUS* "pile", actually!

"Is...is...it enough to buy a building?" asked Max.

"Take another look at the figure. I'd say there's enough to buy fifty buildings. Why you can live just about anyplace you want to now!" said Mr. Fitzbottom, somehow managing to look as if he were the one responsible for all this.

"Well, Moose is still my guardian, isn't he?" said Max.

"I...er...suppose he is," said Mr. Fitzbottom. "But my company will be happy to take on that job now." He gave Max a big, toothy smile.

"I'd rather stick with Moose, if that's okay," said Max. "And we're having an important meeting here right now. So could you come back again tomorrow to talk about this with Moose and me?"

"Shouldn't we...er...ah...um discuss this and settle the matter now?" said Mr. Fitzbottom, winking at Moose. "Don't you agree, Mr. Smith?"

Mr. Smith, otherwise Moose, looked at Max, and shrugged.

"Well, Mr. Smith and I have some decisions to make so we'd rather meet with you about them tomorrow," said Max. "Would ten a.m. be okay?"

"Fine with me," said Moose, swallowing a grin.

"Yes...yes...yes, of course! Ten tomorrow morning it is," said Mr. Fitzbottom.

So the once rotten spoiled obnoxious Maximilian took a deep breath and calmly, coolly held out his hand to take the nervous, sweaty, pudgy hand extended to him.

"Thank you, Mr. Fitzbottom," he said.

Chapter XXV

In which Max learns that there actually are such things as happily-ever-after endings, even when it's not in just a fairy tale.

Mr. Fitzbottom had no sooner bowed himself out the front door, when Max handed Moose the document that Mr. Fitzbottom had left with him.

Moose took a swift look at it.

"Whoo!" he whistled. "If this is for real, and I have every reason to believe that it is, I don't even know what to say."

"Well, you're going to have to say *something*, Moose," said Max. "You're still my guardian, and you're a grown-up, and I'm still just eleven."

Now, all this time the Mother Goose-ites, Mitzi and Mrs. Fiddle, Snitch, and even Moxie and Mojo, had been more or less breathlessly watching the scene at the front door. But the door had no sooner closed behind Mr. Fitzbottom, and they had heard the conversation between Moose and Max, then they all came to life. Mrs. Dumpty was the one who finally spoke up.

"Max is quite right, Moose," she said briskly, "you *are* the grown up, and have to help this poor boy make a decision of some kind, or so it seems. But are we going to be allowed to know what this is all about?"

"Hear! Hear!" said Commander King Cole.

The rest of the Mother Goose-ites all clapped their approval of this idea.

"Okay with you if I tell everyone?" Moose asked Max.

"I want you to," said Max. "Everyone here knows what happened to me and why I'm here. So I think they should know about this as well."

"All right then," said Moose, as soon as he and Max returned to their original places before Mr. Fitzbottom appeared. "It seems that Max has not been left a penniless orphan after all. Well, he's still an orphan, but due to some kind of crazy, unbelievable mix-up, he's now no longer penniless. In fact he's rich as Croesus, if you must know."

There was a collective, excepting Moxie and Mojo, deep breath taken around the room.

"Wow!" said Mitzi.

"Wow, indeed!" said Commander King Cole.

"So what are you thinking about all this, darlin'?" asked Mrs. Dumpty.

"Well...well...well excuse me for interrupting Moose," said Max, "But when I asked Mr. Fitzbottom about buying a building, I sort of had something in mind."

"And what was that, kid?" asked Moose.

"The building I was talking about was Measley Manor," replied Max.

"Why can't I buy it just as well as anyone else?"

"You could," said Moose, "But why would you want to? It wasn't too many days ago that, if I'm not mistaken, you arrived here with your feet dragging. And I had the distinct feeling that you even had plans to run away. So why would you now want to own a home for...um...old wrinkled people who once gave you the creeps?"

"People can change their minds, can't they?" said Max stiffly.

"They can," said Moose.

"Well, I've changed mine, and this is what I want to do, and who's going go stop me?" said Max.

"As your guardian, I could," said Moose.

"Are you going to?" asked Max.

Moose hesitated a moment, and then grinned. "No," he said.

The stunned silence in the room was suddenly broken with cheers and applause.

"Good for you, darlin'!" said Mrs. Dumpty.

"This is wonderful, Max," said Moose, "But who do you think is going to run this place?'

"You," said Max promptly.

"Nice of you to decide my life," said Moose. "But you may have forgotten, I'm a lawyer, not a manager of retirement homes."

"You learned to be a seaman and a handyman, didn't you?" said Max.

"Guess I did," said Moose.

"So you could learn to do this, couldn't you?" said Max.

"Guess I could," said Moose.

"Besides, if I stay here, you have to stay here, too, because you're my guardian, and who knows what kind of stuff I might get into if you're not around to stop me," said Max.

"You're right about that," said Moose.

"The only thing is," said Max, "I'd like it if we can do better than me living in the cellar and you in the garage. We could maybe build us a little house."

"Guess we could do that," said Moose.

"So is it agreed that this is what we're going to tell Mr. Fitzbottom when we meet with him tomorrow?" asked Max.

Moose shrugged and finally grinned. "Okay, kid, if you say so," he said.

"And did anyone ever tell you you'd make quite a salesman?"

With this, the room shook with applause.

When this had died down, Max said, "Oh, and there's a couple of other things. When Delilah returns, I want her to have the title of Head of Housekeeping."

Then Max looked over at Snitch and his bruised face, looking very downcast.

"And," Max continued, "I also want Snitch to be...to be...Chairman In Charge of Cleaning."

"You mean you ain't goin' to fire me?" said Snitch.

"No, why would I?" asked Max.

"Because of the way I been treatin' you, makin' you call me Mr. Snitch and all that," said Snitch. "And because I took this. I only borrowed it. I meant to return it. Honest I did! But I shouldn't o' taken it without askin'."

With that, Snitch crossed the room and handed Max the gold medal from his parents for rescuing the kitten.

"I figured you had it," said Max.

"But you never said nothin'," said Snitch.

Max just shrugged. There was no use now in saying anything, especially seeing Snitch's bruised face and knowing the reason for it.

"An' you still want me to stay and be Chairman in Charge o' Cleanin'?" said Snitch.

"I do," said Max firmly. "Who knows more about cleaning than you do, Snitch? I could never find anybody better anywhere in the world!"

Snitch beamed. "Wow! Chairman in Charge o' Cleanin'! My pa was never Chairman o' Nothin'. Wait 'til he sees what I 'mounted to. But if I got to be keepin' an eye on things here, and you probably ain't goin' to be remainin' in your room, could I move into it?"

"Are you sure you want to?" asked Max.

"Oh, *yes!*" said Snitch, beaming. "I'd put me down a bit o' carpet. Make it real nice. Clean up the washroom, too. Paint it up a bit."

"Oh, but one more thing, Snitch," said Max. "You have to finish high school, too."

"Guess I can work that in," said Snitch. "Wow! Chairman in Charge o' Cleanin'!"

So that final point settled, Max still had something else on his mind.

"I don't want this place to be called Measley Manor any longer. I'm not sure I even want it to be called Dolly Manor. Does anyone have any good ideas about it?"

No one did at the moment. Finally, Max himself broke the silence. "Okay, I have an idea, but I have to consult with someone first."

"Moxie and Mojo, what do you think about this?" he whispered to them.

"*Perfect!*" said Moxie.

"If you'd searched the whole world over, you couldn't have come up with a better name," said Mojo.

So that's how Maximilian Pettigrew Westmorington Bassford Thorndike Finstersill Smith the Fifth, came to be living with Marmaduke Aloisius Smith (otherwise Moose), a girl named Mitzi (with whom he rode to school on a bus because his guardian said going to school - just as with the new Chairman in Charge of Cleaning - was not negotiable), a couple of great mongrels named Moxie and Mojo, and a bunch of very smart people (who just happened to have somehow grown old), in a place called *THE MANOR AT RAINBOW'S END.*

Of course, it was usually only referred to as *THE MANOR,* but everyone knew the story behind it...and knew how things don't always have to gang agley, how skimmed milk can somehow turn to cream, but most importantly, that some stories, bad as they may begin, can somehow turn out to have happily-ever-after fairy tale endings after all!

Barbara Brooks Wallace is an award-winning American children's writer, who was born and spent her childhood in China. She is the winner of two Edgar Allan Poe Awards from the Mystery Writers of America for The Twin in the Tavern (1994) and Sparrows in the Scullery (1998). Cousins in the Castle (1997) and Ghosts in the Gallery (2001) were also nominated for the Edgar Award. She received and the William Allen White Children's Book Award for Peppermints in the Parlor (1983). The trilogy series, Miss Switch, enjoyed a popular run on the successful TV program, The ABC Weekend Specials, garnering the highest Nielsen ratings of all the episodes. Wallace's Hawkins books (which were notable offerings from the elite Scholastic Book Club) were also featured as live action films on The ABC Weekend Specials.

Other Books by
Barbara Brooks Wallace

The Trouble with Miss Switch
Miss Switch to the Rescue
Miss Switch Online
Miss Switch and the Vile Villains
Miss Switch's Bathsheba and the Cat Caper

Dragon for Hire

Diary of a Little Devil
Small Footsteps in the Land of the Dragon